REBEL SQUAD

REBEL SQUAD

PIXIE REBELS™ BOOK TWO

MARTHA CARR
MICHAEL ANDERLE

This book is a work of fiction. All of the characters, organizations, and events portrayed in this novel are either products of the author's imagination or are used fictitiously. Sometimes both.

Copyright © 2023 LMBPN Publishing
Cover by www.mihaelavoicu.com
Cover copyright © LMBPN Publishing
A Michael Anderle Production

LMBPN Publishing supports the right to free expression and the value of copyright. The purpose of copyright is to encourage writers and artists to produce the creative works that enrich our culture.

The distribution of this book without permission is a theft of the author's intellectual property. If you would like permission to use material from the book (other than for review purposes), please contact support@lmbpn.com. Thank you for your support of the author's rights.

LMBPN Publishing
PMB 196, 2540 South Maryland Pkwy
Las Vegas, NV 89109

Version 1.00, March 2023
ebook ISBN: 979-8-88541-955-0
Print ISBN: 979-8-88878-260-6

THE REBEL SQUAD TEAM

Thanks to our JIT Readers

Christopher Gilliard
Peter Manis
Diane L. Smith
Jackey Hankard-Brodie
Dave Hicks
Jan Hunnicutt

CHAPTER ONE

"Are you *sure* it's not too late to go back on our deal?"

Z Thornbrook looked at Domino. "Tell me you're not serious."

He scanned the room where they'd been waiting for about twenty minutes and shrugged.

"You know I'm not, but we'd be *doing* something if we were back on Oriceran instead of stuck waiting in a room. Again."

His sister Echo fixed him with her impassive gaze and punched a fist into her opposite palm. Because there was no one else in the room with them, she was comfortable enough to share her thoughts out loud. "*I'll* give you something to focus on. Like a face sandwich."

"What?" Domino looked from her to Z and wrinkled his nose. "Did you guys learn something new without me?"

"Knuckle sandwich," Z replied with a smirk. "The humans call it a 'knuckle' sandwich."

Echo looked at her fist, turning it over so she could study her knuckles. "Huh."

Domino snickered. "You know, although I like this planet, it's confusing as hell. How does that even make sense? Fist in face equals a sandwich? Where's the bread? What about the mayo?"

Z pointed at him. "I do like mayo."

"Right?"

"I bet if I gave some humans knuckle sandwiches," Echo added in a toneless voice, "I could get at least half of them to tell me what it means."

"Oh, yeah?" Z leaned back in the metal folding chair in front of the desk. "How many humans do you think you'd have to hit to get an explanation?"

"At least a hundred." Echo gazed at the ceiling and narrowed her dark eyes. "Maybe two."

"Sounds like fun." Domino straightened and clapped his hands. "I'm in. When do we start?"

"Yesterday," his sister muttered. "Let's go."

Z closed her eyes and sighed. She knew her cousins' discussion of punching one or two hundred humans in the face was just talk.

With pops, the two pixies disappeared in twin bursts of color. One was dull gray, the other shimmering copper.

Here we go again.

Z joined them, popping in a burst of deep blue before racing after her cousins and zipping in front of them.

Domino and Echo pulled up short and stared at the blue-haired pixie.

With her arms folded, Z blocked her older cousins from the doorknob and cocked her head. "We said we'd wait."

"We've said a lot of things in our lives, Z." Domino

spread his arms. "Did all *those* things happen? Probably not."

"But when we give our *word*?" Z looked from one cousin to the other and adopted a disapproving expression. She hoped it would get the point across. "I thought that meant something."

"I wanna hand out knuckle sandwiches." Echo darted toward the office floor and the sliver of space between it and the bottom of the door.

Z was after her in a flash and pulled up in front of her again. "We're legit now, right? Passed all the tests and everything. There'll be plenty of time for punching people in the face. Later. After we do what we'd said we do and finish waiting, and only if they deserve it."

She pointed at the chairs.

Her cousins exchanged disgruntled looks. Then Domino darted back to where he'd been sitting.

His sister wasn't nearly so eager to give up and wait. Blanking her face, she darted quickly to the right.

Z cut her off in a blur of blue light.

Echo zipped to the left to be off again. In seconds, blurred streaks of gray and blue light were zipping up and down in front of the office door. When she'd had enough, Echo growled in frustration and darted toward the bookshelves at the back of the tiny office. The thick binders and books of regulations stacked on the shelves thumped against each other as she pushed through them to find a hiding place to pout in.

Z sighed. *As soon as we're out of this room, she'll find something else to focus on. Maybe she'll get a few knuckle sandwiches in.*

With another pop, Z resumed the human-sized version of herself, all five feet five inches of it. She stretched her wings behind her and shuddered as she stared at the disrupted bookshelf.

"Echo."

"You're no fun." Her cousin's high-pitched voice emerged from the stack of books, muffled but clearly frustrated.

Z couldn't help snickering. "I *know* you don't mean that."

"Try me."

"No thanks." Z clomped across the linoleum floor to her seat and slumped onto it, making the metal frame squeak. "Trust me. I don't like waiting any more than you guys do."

"You'd rather stay in this cramped room doing nothing just because we *said* we would?" Domino leaned back in his chair, clasped his hands behind his head, and kicked out both legs in front of him. Then he and the entire chair rose four feet in the air and hovered so he could prop his boot heel on the edge of the desk. "Sounds like *somebody's* trying to play both sides of the dollar bill if you ask me."

"I didn't ask you." Trying not to laugh or to look up at him, Z folded her arms and closed her eyes. "And it's both sides of the 'coin.'"

"Well, that's dumb. We should be able to say it however we want." He cocked his head, eyeing her from his elevated position. "Did you find some kinda human-translation book or something? 'Cause that's twice you told us we got the sayings wrong just now. Makes a guy wonder if you've been brushing up on the lingo while he's been asleep."

"No, Dom. I didn't find a human-phrases dictionary."

"Had to ask." He closed his eyes again.

A heavy sigh came from the bookshelf, but nothing more. Echo wasn't ready to rejoin her brother and cousin for their assignment in waiting and more waiting.

This is getting ridiculous, Z thought. *We graduated from training over a week ago, and so far, we've done nothing but wait.*

That was the most frustrating thing about this in-between period. They'd officially completed Basic Training through Major Winters' Oriceran Integration Program, only to be made to wait.

Every time Z thought she might get some time to herself, she and her cousins were interrupted for "one more thing," taken to another room or bay or cramped office, and kept waiting to be assigned a task that ended up taking them five minutes to complete.

"This better be the last time we have to sit around like a bunch of useless worms," Domino murmured.

Z snorted. "*I* can't think of anything else."

"You know what it feels like?" Domino shifted in his chair to look down at her. "Remember that time we were trying to break into that jewelry store, and we kept having to turn back because Bill kept forgetting to bring the right tools?"

"That *was* a pain in the ass, yeah," Z mused.

"The humans are forgetting everything here too. Oh, the pixies need more uniforms? Let's take 'em to another room so they can wait for the guy to take 'em to *another* room so they can wait for the guy who's gonna measure them for uniforms. Awesome."

"Maybe they're just trying to make sure everybody has a job."

"Come on, Z. That's like saying we all need to breathe, so how about we all line up and everybody takes a tiny sliver of a breath one at a time."

Z blinked quickly and tried to figure out how her cousin's mind worked. "I guess."

"Then with the whole *intake* thing, right?" Domino must really be frustrated since he was now voicing *all* his complaints. It didn't matter that his sister and his cousin had been through the same ordeal. "First it's fingerprints. Then no fingerprints. Then off to another room so they can throw lasers at our eyeballs and call it biohazard skinning."

"Wait." She looked up at him, on the verge of laughter. "I think you mean biometric scanning."

"You know exactly what I mean." He stabbed a finger at her and didn't smile. "Whatever it's called, it's just as dumb as everything else they've pulled. Like, they know we can change our eyes whenever we want, just like the rest of us, right?" Domino gestured up and down his body. "Even though this right here is a total work of art."

"Sure, Dom. They know." With another snort, Z closed her eyes again. "Just like they know you're a master of disguise."

"Hey!" Domino leaned over the side of his floating chair, clicked his tongue, and grinned. "I'm flattered, Z. Thanks."

"Ha. Anything to boost your ego, buddy. No problem."

As if that was all he'd wanted to hear, the copper pixie tipped his head over the back of his hovering chair and clasped his hands behind it again. "I guess you're right, though."

"Oh, really?" Z tried to keep a straight face.

"Well, sure. Winters kept his end of the deal, right? We passed the stupid test he gave us at the end of oipcamp, so now we're officially Army soldiers."

"Didn't the major sound *proud* when it happened?"

They both snickered, then Domino said thoughtfully, "I told you I asked him about the smoke, right?"

"What?" Z opened her eyes.

"Sure. Saw him in the hall the other day when I went to the little humans' room. You know, to—"

"I know what a bathroom is, Dom."

"Right. Of course you do. No idea why the guy acted like he didn't wanna talk to me. New oip soldier and all that. He should've at least *acted* proud. I asked him about the smoke."

Z waited for her cousin to continue. When he didn't, she asked, "What *about* the smoke?"

"Oh. You know, what he did to it to make it so easy for us to blast through. Not like I'm complaining, but after that last test, I kept thinking about that time on Oriceran when we were goofing around in that wizard's cabin. Remember his fireplace? The one with all the—"

The bookshelf thumped, and the books shuddered against each other as Echo burst from her hiding place. She darted over to hover above the desk.

"We burned that shit to the ground!" she screeched, her arms spread wide above her, ending in fists of victory.

Z and Domino stared at her, then burst out laughing.

"Hard to forget," Z finally said. "Especially the look on his face!"

"Like he wanted to kill us and *then* himself when…when all his little experiments went up in…purple flames!" Domino spat between bouts of laughter.

The pixies enjoyed the memory a moment longer. Even Echo, who had a hint of a knowing smile at the corners of her mouth. With a contented sigh, Domino shook his head and tipped his chair back. "We had some good times on that planet. You know, before…"

"Yeah," Z replied wistfully. "I'm good with the memories, thanks." She shot her cousin a curious look. "I'm guessing the major didn't have much to say about the smoke, huh?"

"Nope. Couldn't even tell me why it was much easier to blast it all away on *this* planet with a bunch of blind soldiers behind us. But hey, winners can't be losers, right?"

Z didn't bother to correct yet another misunderstood human phrase. She did, however, wonder about the smoke thing too. Now that she thought about it, three pixies blasting away the thick, acrid black smoke *had* been a hell of a lot easier than she'd expected.

She hadn't been thinking about anything but finishing their "training" so they could get out of oipcamp and start doing *something* with their time on Earth. Unfortunately, their time on Earth didn't belong to them anymore. For the duration of their contract as OIP soldiers, they owed their time, dedication, service, and apparently their lives to the United States Army.

That was what it said on the paper, at any rate.

What was with the smoke thing? Winters would not *make anything easy for us. Not on purpose, anyway.*

"What did he say?" she asked.

Domino looked down at her. "Who?"

"*Winters*, Dom!"

"Oh, yeah. He told me to quit wasting his time and go ask someone else a bunch of stupid questions. Couldn't find anyone else in the hall right then, though, and there was nobody else in the crapper. I checked."

Z wrinkled her nose at the thought of her cousin checking the stalls in the restroom. She was interrupted when Echo shot down and plunked on the edge of the desk. She popped into her human-sized form, still sitting on the edge of the desk with one leg crossed, and stared at her brother. "Next time, take me with you."

"To the crapper?" Domino grimaced. "Come on, Echo. That's *too* weird even for you."

The goth slammed a fist into her opposite palm. "I'll *make* him answer you."

"You know what?" Domino pointed at her. "You'd make a great bouncer. That'd totally throw everyone off, right? Does the Army have nightclubs?"

The office was silent after that. Then Z asked the question she'd been silently asking herself about the smoke. "It's probably just thicker on Oriceran."

"What, the nightclubs?" Dom asked.

Echo punched her hand again. "Major Winters' face?"

Z laughed. "The *smoke*. You know what? You guys sound like a broken record."

"I think you mean 'sticky merry-go-round,'" Domino

corrected incorrectly. "But I'm willing to overlook it this one time."

All three heard footsteps outside the office door and the squeak when someone turned the doorknob and opened the door.

The man didn't bother to knock first, so he found one goth punching her palm, one chuckling dude with copper wings dropping in a chair from four feet in the air while jerking his boots off the desk, and one woman with short blue hair throwing her head back with a groan of frustration that didn't sound feigned.

All four legs of Domino's metal chair clanged on the floor. He grunted after the abrupt landing.

"Well, it's about *time*, Major," Z called before turning to face the door. "We were really starting to wonder if you... are *not* the major."

Domino spun, grinning as he looked the newcomer over. "Whoa. Nice facelift, Major. You look great!"

The man who was not Major Winters clamped his mouth shut and cleared his throat. He glared at Domino. "If you can't tell the difference between your CO and your escort, you're gonna have a real problem getting outta here."

"Hey, you know who you look like now?" Domino continued, shaking a thoughtful finger at the much younger uniformed person. "Aw, man. It's right on the tip of my— That's it! Sergeant Balsam. *That's* who you look like."

The sergeant's only reaction was to blink a few times in disbelief. Then he turned his attention to Z. "Is he for real?"

She looked the man over and shrugged. "Are *you*?"

Echo returned to pixie size, darted toward her brother, and resized right beside him.

Balsam took a step back in surprise. "What is she doing?"

The goth leaned down to whisper in her brother's ear, and Domino grinned. "You're so right." He turned to the NCO who'd come to fetch them. "She says you really shouldn't try to take on someone else's identity. That's *my* thing."

"Holy shit." Sergeant Balsam shook his head. "I'm *so* ready to be done with this shit."

"Where is he?" Z asked as her cousins scrutinized the sergeant. They'd only seen him a few times during their stay. "The major, I mean. He was supposed to come get us and take us wherever we're going next. I think."

"Not my job to know or care." Balsam stepped out of the cramped office and gestured down the hall with a sweep of his arm. "Just gotta get you three to the next step. Let's move."

"You're not even a *little* worried about him?" She clicked her tongue as she stood. "That's pretty reckless if you ask me, but okay."

"Z," Domino whispered loud enough for everyone to hear as he stood. "Why is Major Winters acting like someone else?"

She shrugged. "Ask *him*."

Her cousin glanced at the sergeant, then shook his head and waved it off. "Nah. I don't wanna crush his confidence. Not first thing in the morning."

"I said move," Balsam snapped, and all three human-sized pixies strode casually out of the room.

The sergeant watched them, still shaken by the sight of three normal-looking people in uniform with wings sprouting from their backs. He shook his head and peered into the cramped office in which the pixies had been waiting just in case.

A book fell off the bookshelf and hit the floor with a thump, but that was it.

With a grimace, Sergeant Balsam closed the door and took off after the Army's newest, and by far strangest, recruits.

CHAPTER TWO

"Take a seat," Balsam grumbled, ushering Z and her cousins into yet another room.

This one was much larger than the first and held a large table. Domino approached the circular table and eyed the packets of paper on it, each with a pen beside it. He looked at the sergeant and murmured, "You forgot the nametags."

"Pick a chair. Sit in it. Fill that out." Balsam pointed at the packets of papers, then folded his arms. "You have one hour."

"For what?" Z asked as she moved toward one of the packets.

"It's another test. And yeah, the answers *do* matter, so don't screw around when you're filling that out."

"Ooh! Do we get prizes afterward?" Domino plopped into his seat and grinned at the sergeant.

The man looked like he was ready to give up. He stared blankly at the pixies and didn't say another word.

"Looks like the clock's ticking," Z remarked as she took a seat. "I just hope nobody expected us to study for this."

"If it's a test about human sayings that confuse the hell outta me, you'll win." Domino dropped an elbow on the table and put his chin in his hand. "I hate tests."

Having sat at a third point around the circular table, Echo was flipping through the packet of test papers. With the tip of her tongue poking from the corner of her mouth and one eye narrowed, she scribbled furiously on the test, occasionally pausing to pay special attention to whatever question had caught her up.

Z and Domino watched her briefly, then exchanged knowing looks and shrugged.

"I take it back," Domino muttered. "Echo wins."

"No talking," Balsam interrupted. "And don't tell me you have no idea how tests work."

"Huh." Z gazed at the ceiling and tapped the end of her pen on her chin. "You know what? I can't remember the last time I took a test. Not on paper, anyway."

Domino's hand shot into the air. When the sergeant understandably didn't call on him, the copper pixie blurted, "What if I have to go to the bathroom? Like, really bad."

"Uh-oh." Z scanned the first page. "Looks like somebody's got test anxiety."

"Sergeant?" Domino waved his hand urgently as if the room were full of people and he had to try doubly hard to get his escort's attention.

There was no way for Sergeant Balsam *not* to notice the copper pixie, but he tried his damnedest to pretend he didn't see or hear a thing.

Domino started bouncing and fidgeting in his chair,

grimacing and letting out little disturbed grunts as he waved his arm.

"Jesus Christ, Boot," Balsam finally growled before gesturing harshly toward the door. "This isn't kindergarten. If you gotta go, fucking go and come back."

Domino froze and gave the sergeant a lopsided smile. "Cool. Thanks."

He turned back to his test and looked at the first page.

Despite all his efforts to remain detached from the recruits for whom he was temporarily responsible, Balsam couldn't ignore the potential accident—and no doubt the ensuing mess—if one pixie in particular didn't get a handle on his bodily functions. "Well, aren't you gonna go?"

"Huh?" The pixie glanced at his escort as if their previous conversation hadn't happened. "Oh. Nah, I'm good. Just wanted to make sure I know how this works."

Domino dove back into his test, his forehead propped in one hand while he read the questions before scribbling down his answers.

Sergeant Balsam forced himself not to scream obscenities at the copper pixie for wasting his time. When he got his irritation under control, he watched the recruits take their tests.

At first, it looked like they were being good little soldiers, intent on doing what was required of them.

The seconds ticked by. The room was uncharacteristically silent.

Too silent.

Balsam didn't know these three recruits very well. As backup operations support for a very small, incredibly strange secret Army program, he didn't encounter them much, but even he knew this kind of meticulous silence was not normal.

It made him jumpy.

Like the calm before the storm, he thought, trying not to stare at the three pixies scribbling on their tests. *And I'm the only asshole in the room with them. Alone. Shit.*

He glanced at his watch and felt even worse about the situation when he realized it had only been ten minutes since he'd started their one-hour timer.

Fifteen minutes in, a sheen of nervous sweat had broken out on his forehead. He forced himself not to wipe it away since there was no way in hell he was going to let these three magical assclowns see that he was having a hard time spending an hour alone with them.

To make matters worse, the pixies were being model soldiers, at least for test-taking.

At the twenty-two-minute mark, Echo scribbled the last of her answers, slammed her pen on the table with a bang that startled the sergeant, shoved back in her chair, and folded her arms. The metal chair legs screeched noisily across the floor, but the other two pixies gave no indication of noticing.

Balsam glanced at his watch again and frowned.

Without looking up from his test, Domino pointed across the table at his sister and murmured, "She says she's done."

"She didn't say anything," the sergeant replied.

"Sure she did. You just gotta know how to read between the lines."

"Between the…" Balsam hissed through his teeth. "*What* lines?"

"Wow. Just my luck." Domino calmly turned to the next page of his test. "I know I got that human saying right, but I said it to the most literal human who's ever walked the planet. You know how that makes me feel? Like giving up. Maybe you should give up too, Sergeant. You know, if you're so intent on making things so difficult for everyone around you."

"Difficult?" Balsam gave a bitter laugh. "I'll show you difficult. *You're* the one waltzing your magical ass in here and thinking you can tell everybody what they—"

"Shh!" Z set both forearms on the table and looked up. "Sergeant, *please*. Some of us are trying to focus on our *tests* if you don't mind."

The man blinked, realizing he'd been clenching his fists. He found it irritating that Domino hadn't even looked at him during their brief but exasperating excuse for a conversation.

He did, however, both see and feel the blue-haired pixie's gaze on him, which was clearly meant to make him feel like crap for breaking her concentration.

It didn't. It *did* remind him of why he was here, which wasn't to get involved in the maddening conversations with three insane magical rejects who had somehow managed to complete their brief and incredibly unorthodox training.

He folded his arms again, then glanced around the room and cleared his throat because Z still hadn't returned her attention to her test.

What does she want from me? An apology? Fat chance.

He gazed back with what he hoped was an impassive expression.

Apparently, that was all she wanted. She returned to her test and the hard work of reading and answering questions. It didn't escape his notice when she murmured an exasperated, "*Thank* you."

Goddamn, I can't wait for these little cretins to get the hell out of here so I can go back to my regular life. Worst assignment I've had since Basic. Hell, this might even be worse *than Basic.*

Echo sat with her arms folded, glaring across the table at her brother and her cousin. Every so often, the other pixies would briefly meet her gaze before returning to the task at hand.

At forty-five minutes, Sergeant Balsam's cell phone buzzed. The sound came from his pants pocket, and though it was the opposite of loud and obnoxious, all three pixies fixed him with disapproving stares.

"Don't look at *me*," Balsam grumbled as he pulled his phone out of his pocket. He nodded at the table. "Focus."

As he walked across the room to the farthest corner for privacy, Domino leaned toward his cousin and whispered, "Hey, Z."

"Uh-huh." She kept scribbling and didn't look at him.

"What'd you put down for Number Twenty-five?"

Z paused, flipped back through the last few pages of the test to check her answer, and murmured, "I said, 'Live and let live. Or burn the whole thing down. One or the other.'"

"Ooh, yeah. That's good." Domino sat upright and tapped his pen on his temple with a lazy smile. "Give 'em *options*."

He looked at his sister, who was now busily drawing lopsided smiley faces in the air with threads of silver light.

One of them wobbled across the table toward Domino,

and he chuckled before clicking his tongue and shooting Echo a quick wink. "You've got this on lock, E. I feel it in my guts. All of them."

The goth's expression remained unchanged, but she flicked her finger at the wobbly smiley face and sent a wave of shuddering air coursing across the table. The smiley face wobbled even more, then the smile morphed into a mouth gaping in horror before the silver light dissipated.

Looking like she was still paying attention to her test, Z smirked as she wrote down and checked off more answers.

"What about this one?" Domino stabbed a finger at his current page. "'What do you do if you see your commanding officer engaging in misconduct?' That seems like a loaded question."

"I think they're all loaded questions, Dom," Z replied. "Just like the guns."

"Huh. So you're saying the trick is knowing how and when to pull the trigger."

"Hey!" Sergeant Balsam barked and strode across the room to take up his previous position. "This isn't Happy Hour. No talking."

Domino let out a giggle. "Two things that should never be in the same room at the same time. Kindergarten and Happy Hour."

"He keeps telling us what this *isn't*," Z added under her breath. "Makes me wonder if he has any idea what it *is*."

"I think the sergeant needs to make up his mind."

"I know you heard me," Balsam snapped, then pointed at Echo. "And don't think I didn't see that little glowy thing with the lights you just did. Trust me, the last thing I wanna do is make all three of you start over, but if I catch any of you cheating, that's exactly what I'll do."

"Are we getting graded on this, Sergeant?" Z asked.

"Aw, *man!*" Domino slumped closer to his test, looking dejected, then glanced at his cousin. "Is *that* the prize? I've never gotten *any* grades."

"Hey, you'll get one eventually," Z added in mock reassurance. "Just keep doing your best. That's all they want."

"It's never *enough!*" Domino wailed and thumped a fist on the table. "Some of us just aren't cut out for tests."

"Last warning, Private," Balsam barked, then scrunched his face since his words had confused even him.

Jesus Christ! I'm calling him "private," and I don't have a damn clue what rank these little shits hold. Do they even have *a rank?*

While Sergeant Balsam tried to figure out how he was supposed to address the pixies—he had a feeling "asshole," "maggot," or "shithead" would get him a hefty dose of magical blowback he didn't know how to handle—Domino's uncomfortable fidgeting increased.

The copper pixie flipped through the pages of his test with renewed urgency, going from one question to the other and scanning what he'd written.

Z forced herself not to look at him as she finished the last question in her packet, though she was watching him from the corner of her eye.

"Shit," Domino murmured. "Hey, Sergeant?"

"*What?*" Balsam groaned.

"What's my time?"

The sergeant gave Domino a blank stare.

"Come on, Sergeant. My *time*. What's my—" The copper

pixie froze to eye his cousin as Z closed her finished test packet, turned it over, and set her pen beside it. "Aw, *man*! How'd you do that so fast?"

Z shrugged and sat back. "It's just a test."

"Just a test. Just a *test*? Great Crabby Chrismister, Z. It's never 'just a test.'"

"A little one, Dom." She held her thumb and forefinger close together to emphasize her point. "A tiny test."

Her cousin shot her another glance, and they pressed their lips together to keep from cracking up. Domino got enough control of himself to dive back into his faux panic, then slammed both hands on the table and spun in his chair. "Sergeant, *please!*"

"Jesus." Balsam checked his watch. "Nine minutes."

"Nine minutes. *Nine*. Aw, come on! The *pressure*." Domino dropped his head into his hand and pouted for the next three minutes without breaking character or saying another word.

Sergeant Balsam started to look worried about the copper pixie's mental state, and he gave Z a questioning look.

She raised her eyebrows and shrugged.

With six minutes left, Domino sprang out of his nearly catatonic contemplation and raced through the rest of the test. The frantic scratching of his pen was the only sound in the otherwise silent room as he shook his head and muttered nonsense under his breath.

"I can't take it." He slammed his pen on the table and shouted, "Will somebody turn off that *ticking*?"

Echo snapped her fingers.

Domino straightened in his chair, cocked his head, and let out a noisy sigh of relief. "So much better."

While the goth's response did nothing and wasn't meant to have any effect on her brother, its effect on Sergeant Balsam was clear…and intended.

The sergeant took a step back, frowning as he scanned the room for a ticking clock.

Z's ability to keep her amusement hidden failed. She snickered before dipping her head.

Domino's gonna break the guy during a test. That might be a new record.

Her cousin continued scribbling on the last page, then slammed the table again. "*Done!*"

His pen skittered across the table toward Echo, who flicked the air to send the writing instrument rolling back toward him.

"I'm done, Sergeant," Domino called as he spun his chair. Both hands shot up as he stared at the NCO. "Done. I did it. Finished. What's my time?"

Balsam's mouth opened and closed. He'd been thoroughly caught up in the copper pixie's mad scramble.

"Sergeant, I need to know!"

"Uh, it's… You're…" The man finally remembered to look at his watch and shouted, "One minute seven seconds!"

The tension in the room was palpable as all three pixies waited for the sergeant's next move and Balsam waited for the terrifying reaction he was expecting. When he swallowed, his throat emitted an audible click.

Echo cocked her head.

"Sergeant?" Z asked. "You feeling okay?"

"Uh-oh." Domino exaggerated a grimace. "Do *you* need to go? Like, really bad? You're sweating all over your—"

"I'm not telling you shit." Balsam shook his head like he was trying to clear the memory of the last several minutes, then stalked toward the table and pointed at the tests. "I'll take those."

"Sure." Z leaned back in her chair and lifted both hands in concession. When the NCO realized she wasn't going to hand him her packet, he swiped the test off the table and headed for Domino.

"Here you go, Sergeant." The copper pixie held his test out with enthusiasm. "Can't wait to get my prize."

Balsam snatched it out of his hand and continued around the table toward Echo, who shoved her test packet toward him. It fluttered across the table, flapping and turning over before landing at the very edge. The sergeant looked at her in irritation, but the reaction he got out of her was no different from what everyone else got—a blank, soulless stare that made the hairs on the back of his neck stand on end.

He managed to push past the discomfort to grab her messy packet and slammed it on top of the disheveled pile in his hands, then stepped away from the table. He kept eyeing the pixies like he expected them to pounce on him and rip him apart.

"Don't go anywhere," he muttered. Torn between his military training and the unfamiliar sensation of walking away from three aggravating—and possibly insane—magicals, Balsam left the room. He hoped he'd saved his dignity, but he really didn't want to turn his back on them.

When he reached the door, his resolve abandoned him.

He fumbled with the doorknob, threw open the door, and booked it without bothering to close that door behind hm. The NCO's footsteps echoed into the room as he raced down the hall, leaving the pixies alone.

"Well." Domino tossed his hands in the air and let them flop down at his sides in exasperation. "Guess I'm not the only one with text anxiety."

The pixies' laughter overpowered the fading echo of Sergeant Balsam's bootsteps.

CHAPTER THREE

A different NCO came to fetch Z and her cousins from the "test room." Sergeant Kayley wouldn't explain where he was taking them, why Sergeant Balsam hadn't returned, and where Major Winters was or answer anything else the pixies asked as he led them through multiple winding corridors. He stopped in front of an unmarked door and pulled out a jangling set of keys.

"Oh, boy." Domino did a little dance. "It's everything I've ever wanted, Sergeant. How did you *know?*"

"The only thing I know is that you need somewhere to hang tight and that *this* room is available."

"Wow." The copper pixie rubbed his disheveled hair and exaggerated a grimace. "Sounds like a super boring life if those are the *only* two things you know. Hey, don't worry about your name, though, Sergeant. We got that one covered."

Kayley shook his head, trying to find the right one for the door he'd chosen.

"Wait, what *is* your name? Oh. Shit." Domino snapped

his fingers and pointed at the sergeant. "Not one of the things you know."

Kayley had better control of his irritation than Sergeant Balsam and said nothing. The lock finally gave, and the door swung open. Beyond it was another cramped office like the first one, save that this one didn't have three extra chairs smooshed together for the troublemaking trio of pixies.

The only chair in it sat behind a small desk just large enough to hold an old, clunky desktop computer, an equally old and clunky receptionist's phone, and a tiny desk lamp.

Z peered past Kayley and raised an eyebrow. "What was wrong with the other room?"

"What other room?"

"The one you just got us out of?" She smiled and cocked her head. "Come on, Sergeant. That was only, like, five minutes ago."

"Z," Domino muttered, "he only knows *two things*."

"Nothing wrong with the other room," Kayley stated as he pulled the key from the doorknob. He stepped back and gestured inside, "Or this one."

"Except that it's way smaller."

"Huh. Yeah." The sergeant stroked his beardless chin and nodded thoughtfully. "Well then, why don't you shrink yourself *real* small and make more room, huh? That should be pretty easy for ya."

"Ooh, *boy*." Grimacing, Domino glanced between his cousin and the one NCO they'd met who felt like testing the waters with his attitude. "I can *hear* the cajónes on this guy."

Z folded her arms and glowered at Kayley. "He's got somethin' on him, all right. And I'd still love to know why we couldn't keep hanging out in the big, roomy office instead of getting kicked into the closet again."

The sergeant held his ground. "I bet you would."

"Wanna make another bet?" Z stepped toward him and raised her chin, then realized she was pushing it. Her growing frustration over the last week wasn't Sergeant Kayley's fault, but like every other time Z's anger had gotten the better of her, it was hard to snuff out the fire after the spark had been lit.

"Let's start with how happy Major Winters'll be when he hears you *encouraged* three new recruits to act like pixies rather than soldiers. Is that what you want?"

"Watch it, Boot." Kayley's eyes narrowed, but that was his only reaction. Clearly, the man had been briefed on everyday interactions with the pixies.

"You can tell him whatever you want. Normally, that's called breaking rank, but I don't think anyone here gives a shit. I was told to take the three of you somewhere else, and this is somewhere else, so sit down and shut up."

Z's knuckles cracked when she clenched her fists, but the expression on the sergeant's face mirrored the one she wore when she didn't care if the other party had steam coming out of their ears.

This was a lost cause.

Would punching a sergeant in the face for no good reason other than I really *want to be grounds for getting us kicked out? Probably.*

"Sit where, exactly?" Domino piped as he leaned around his cousin to peer into the office. "There's nothing in here."

"That's the point. Move it." Kayley glanced at his watch, then gestured for them to enter again.

Even though she was aware of what a bad idea it would be to continue the standoff, Z couldn't bring herself to carry out his instruction. Her feet wouldn't move, and her burning glare remained firmly fixed on the sergeant's apathetic face.

While their cousin simmered like a ticking pixie time-bomb, Domino and Echo shared a knowing look. They didn't have to talk about how to keep this section of the facility from erupting in blue magical rage. Domino pointed down the hall and shouted, "Holy shit! What's *that?*"

They hadn't officially entered a staring contest, but Sergeant Kayley lost anyway when he broke from Z's gaze to turn his head in that direction. He was clearly unimpressed by the juvenile tactic. "I can't believe this is an actual fucking conversation."

When the man's attention wasn't directed at Z, Echo zipped in front of her cousin to stand between the sergeant and his demise if nobody intervened.

At the same time, Dom zapped Z in the ribs with copper light. "Oh, it's there all right, Sergeant. I *swear* I saw something."

Z blinked furiously and sucked in a sharp breath as the magic jolt did what it was supposed to do: rip her out of her growing fury. She turned her glare on the copper pixie instead. "What's *your* problem?"

"Just get in the damn office," Sergeant Kayley snapped when he decided he'd had enough of them.

"Yep." Domino grabbed Z by the shoulders and tossed

her in. "We're on it like wings on pixies, Sergeant. Like eggs on toast. Like...black on Echo."

"I swear to God," Kayley muttered as he turned back to the pixies and the open door. "Someone had to drop you on your head as a baby. And *you*. Quit standing there just—"

He stopped when he realized the woman in front of him was not the one with short blue hair and blue wings but the goth. A sneer curled his lip. "Took your bait-and-switch skills straight from a cartoon, huh?"

Echo thrust her index and middle finger toward her eyes, then pointed them at him. Her expression never changed.

"I totally get how you'd come to that conclusion," Domino called from inside the office as he struggled to keep Z inside.

Although she repeatedly slapped his hands, hissing in irritation and trying to get away, the copper pixie had moved her farther into the room. It hadn't been subtle.

"I'd be doing all of us a...*ow*. A serious disservice if I...*stop*," he hissed at Z like she was a toddler tugging too forcefully on his arm, then managed to finish his sentence. "If I didn't correct the misconception. Nobody picks us up as babies, sergeants. Or catches us. Or drops us."

Kayley blinked in confusion and shook his head.

As Echo walked backward toward the open door, Domino leaned sideways to peer around his sister while trying to keep Z's flailing hands restrained. "We hatch."

"The fuck?" The sergeant wasn't able to keep up with the conversation or the distracting actions of all three pixies as they did what he'd told them to do.

"From eggs." Domino flashed the man a quick grin and a nod.

Kayley's frown deepened. He looked more like an adolescent who'd been blindsided by the birds-and-bees talk than an NCO trying to corral three pixies into a cramped office because those were his orders. "Jesus! I don't need to know about that shit."

"I wouldn't run around talking about what did and didn't happen to us as babies if you don't wanna hear the truth," Domino shot back. "Misinformation is a dangerous thing, Sergeant."

"What?" Kayley took a quick step forward. "Don't talk to me about mis—"

"Listen, I'd love to keep this little chat going, but we're *really* busy in here. Maybe another time." Domino didn't take his eyes off the NCO, even when Z finally broke free of his grasp and charged toward the door. "Thanks for stopping by, Sergeant. Have a great day. *Bye.*"

Echo grabbed the door and slammed it in Sergeant Kayley's face. After it was closed, she spun to shoot her cousin a deadpan stare of disapproval and warning. Z realized she wouldn't step back through it anytime soon.

Kayley had the same thought on the other side. It had been a long time since anyone had interrupted or corrected him or slammed a door in his face. All three of those things had just been thrown at him by a goth chick and a dude who looked like every other regular-Joe soldier except for the copper wings sprouting from his back.

It took longer than usual for him to comprehend what had happened.

The scuffles, thumps, and harsh whispers from inside

the office brought him back to reality and reminded him *he* was the NCO and *they* were new recruits. He didn't give a shit what they thought of him as long as they did what they were told.

Which they had.

Knowing these three new magical recruits had followed his orders without putting up much of a fight in the pixie scheme of things didn't make Sergeant Kayley feel like he could write this off as a job well done.

It unnerved him.

He fiddled with the keyring in his hand until he found the right key. As he slid it into the lock, he sighed and shook his head. "More like misdirection. In all the wrong places. How did anyone think this was a good fucking idea?"

After he'd locked the door, he jiggled the knob to make sure, then stepped back and stared at the door for another second. After that, he spun on his heel and marched down the hall, shaking his head the whole time.

CHAPTER FOUR

Inside the cramped office, the three pixies heard Sergeant Kayley lock the door.

Domino glared at the closed door in disbelief. "Oh, come on! They still think locks are gonna do anything?"

Whether it was her cousin's frustration at the lack of knowledge concerning pixie abilities or the fact the first target of her anger was now out of sight but not yet out of mind, Z turned her frustration elsewhere.

The closest target was Domino.

With a growl, the blue-haired pixie slammed a fist into his ribs. The flash of blue light upon contact sent Domino flying across the office.

His back bashed into the opposite wall, and several binders toppled off the shelf above him. One bounced off his head and hit the floor. Another headed for the same target, but Echo blasted it with a streak of silver light that ripped the binder in half and scattered loose papers all over the office and the desk.

Domino was aware of his sister's save, but he kept his attention on Z as he rubbed his ribs and muttered, "Ow."

Folding her arms, Z stalked toward the back wall. If the space had been bigger, she might have been able to blow off steam, but this room only allowed her to take five steps in that direction. Then she had to turn and take ten steps toward the opposite wall.

"What was *that* for?" Domino shouted, looking at his ribs to assess the damage.

There wasn't any damage since Z would never hurt her own flesh and blood. Not badly, anyway. Z wasn't able to look at either of her cousins as she angrily paced across the crowded space.

"You hit her first," Echo answered with a shrug. "I expected her to hit you back even harder."

"Hit me back?" Domino looked clueless about the point his sister had just made. Then he remembered that Z excelled at one-upping anyone who pissed her off. "Fine. I admit I should've seen that coming."

"Yup," his sister murmured.

He shot her a quick warning glance, then returned his attention to Z. "But we had to stop you from making some serious mistakes out there. That sergeant isn't worth it. None of them are."

"I wasn't gonna do anything," Z grumbled as she pivoted to stalk away from them again.

"Hmm. Echo, you smell that?" Domino wafted his hand in front of his face before turning a questioning gaze on his sister.

Echo sniffed at the air, then shrugged.

"Yeah, it's coming to me now." He stared contemplatively at the ceiling, then looked curtly at Z and raised his eyebrows. "That's the smell of cow shit."

"Bullshit," Echo corrected.

"Whatever. It's the same thing. *You* know what I mean." He pointed at Z again.

When she didn't stop pacing or bother to look at him, Domino let out a heavy sigh. A blast of copper light streamed from his finger and darted in front of his cousin's face before bursting against the office wall beside her head.

That made her stop and look at him with a mask of apathy that almost matched Echo's. Z blinked, then muttered, "You missed."

"No, I was aiming for the wall." Domino put both hands on his hips, which made him look like one of the Thornbrook elders from their childhood.

The resemblance was so startling that it knocked Z out of her bubbling anger. All thoughts of Sergeant Kayley and what she might or might not have done to him vanished.

Like their family.

We're the only ones left. What are we doing fighting with each other?

Z sighed. "You look just like Pappy."

Domino looked at her, then down at himself in an attempt to see what she was seeing.

Echo closed one eye and held her thumb and forefinger toward her brother, squinting through the space between her fingers to play with the visual perspectives. Then she slammed her fingers together and mimicked the sound of an explosion that was remarkably accurate.

He fixed his sister with a disapproving scowl. "You

realize there's a point where you take being morbid way too far, right?"

"Not really."

Z looked at her cousins. *If she needs to make jokes about our entire family dying without saying anything, who are we to tell her to stop? It's not like we've sat down and talked about it since leaving Oriceran.*

When her memory took a dark turn toward the fateful night none of them were willing to revisit, she shook her head to clear the thoughts away. "I know I didn't hurt you," Domino flicked his gaze toward Z as she continued, "But I'm sorry anyway."

Her cousins stared at her in disbelief, then Domino's hands dropped. "Shit."

"Better write that down," Echo said flatly, "Or take a picture. Anyone got a camera?"

Domino and Z ignored her. Z tried not to fidget, but it was hard when all three pixies felt the tension, and all three knew exactly why it was there.

Okay, I'm not big on apologies. I get it. We don't need to make a big deal out of it.

Instead of saying it out loud, she continued pacing.

It didn't feel nearly as productive as it had when she was trying to find an outlet for her anger, but it was the only thing she could do.

Her cousins watched her, then exchanged knowing looks. Domino ran a hand through his messy copper hair. "All right, Z. What gives?"

"Take your pick," she muttered without looking at him.

"I mean with *you*. You were ready to pick a fight with Sergeant Dropped-You-On-Your-Head out there, and then you picked a fight with *me*. Not that I couldn't have handled it."

"She would've crushed you like a worm," Echo murmured with a flicker of a smile.

"That's not the point," her brother finished, ignoring her. "Like, at all. So, what's going on with you?"

It took a minute for Z to figure out what she wanted to say. Whenever her anger flared, ready to unleash itself all over whoever was standing in her way, she didn't have the time or the focus to pinpoint the *reason* for that anger.

It had come on faster than she'd expected in the hallway.

I have to talk about it, or I'm gonna get us all tossed back to Oriceran when I promised them I'd look out for them. For all of us.

Z kicked aside the rickety office chair. It scooted away from the desk, showing off the tattered edges of the cloth seat and one broken armrest. Pulling it back, she slumped into the worn seat with a heavy sigh, then kicked the chair back. It rolled over the papers scattered across the floor. The back wheels clanged against the edge of a metal bookshelf against the wall, which stopped her.

She could feel her cousins' curious and concerned gazes but couldn't look at them. She couldn't find anything better to say than, "I hate wasting time."

"Yeah. Right." Domino folded his arms and cocked his head. "You realize how much time we've wasted since we started this whole pixies-in-the-Army thing, right? And that shit was *fun*."

Echo raised a finger in the air. "I'd do it again, but with more screaming and a lot more blood. Obviously."

That made Z snort. Domino grinned at her and approached the desk. "Especially in the last couple days. So much wasted time. Not nearly as much fun, but hey, when they want to test geniuses like us on paper over and over, fine. We'll show them geniuses."

Z finally looked at her cousin and managed a smirk. "Geniuses like us, huh? They'll have to reinvent the definition. Echo answered all her multiple-choice questions with a smiley face."

The goth shrugged, her expression as unchanging and unreadable as ever. "Aced it."

"Well, duh." Domino winked at his sister, then resumed his caregiving air and lifted one leg to sit sideways on the edge of the desk. "Which makes your answer even more of a crappy attempt not to answer."

Z could feel the urgency, concern, and amusement from both cousins. She wanted to say something useful but still didn't know why she'd been so angry or was so bothered by this next stage of Army processing to their real work, whatever *that* meant.

"I don't know," she muttered, figuring it was better to work it out by talking since not saying anything about it wasn't going well for her or any of the pixies. "I guess it's… I mean, if they aren't gonna *do* anything with us right now, what's the point of moving us around every couple of hours to do more nothing?"

Domino chuckled. "Maybe it's additional training. Like, 'Hey, now you guys get to get *really* good at absolutely nothing, so hurry up and wait.' That sounds pretty accurate."

"Sounds like death," Echo murmured. "Race, race, race.

Everybody work hard and do stuff and go faster and be better so you can drop dead at the last second and then just disappear."

Z and Domino looked at her in surprise, then he snorted and shook his head. "You're saying the Army's death."

Echo rolled her eyes and shrugged. "Death might be better at this point."

"Damn." Her brother's crooked smile was mixed with concern. It flickered, and he turned back to Z. "Don't let *them* hear you say that, huh?"

Z let out a wry chuckle. "If you're asking *my* opinion, Dom, the jury's still out."

"Ha. Right." Domino nodded, then cocked his head and frowned. "Where'd they go?"

Z continued working through her thoughts aloud. "I'd rather be doing *something* with all this downtime than sitting around and getting pissed about it."

Like finally opening that letter with the Oriceran symbol stamped on it. Zero humans should have anything to do with that. I haven't had anywhere near enough time to sit down and go through it. We keep getting called away for nothing.

Domino looked confused as he tried to figure out the latest human saying, but she knew he was still listening. Echo had resorted to picking the nonexistent dirt out from under her nails, but she was listening, too.

Despite Z being the youngest, the siblings always listened to what she had to say. She got them out of every pickle they got themselves into, and that included the US Army.

"Here's what gets me," Z added, swiveling back and

forth in the office chair. It let out a shrill squeak of protest with every turn. "I wanna know when they're going to let us do what we want with our free time instead of dictating that to us like they dictate everything else."

Domino scoffed. "You know what Major Winters would say to that?"

Z scrunched her face into an impersonation of the major and lowered her voice. *"This is the Army."*

Echo hissed.

With a crooked smile, Domino tipped his head back and forth as he remembered the major's face when he was telling the pixies where they were. "That's *exactly* what he'd say and everything that comes with it. He only covered us having to eat, sleep, breathe, and shit where he tells us while we were *in training*, and that's over." He paused, frowning. "Honestly, that last part's still confusing. He *never* told me where to shit."

Z punched a fist into her palm. "Well, now he's telling us where we can and can't get a damn break from all this...this..."

"Existential limbo," Echo muttered.

Frowning at her cousin, Z shook her head. "That wasn't what I was going for, but I guess it works."

"What would you rather be doing right now?" Domino asked as he stroked his chin. "It looks like you've got something in mind."

"I don't know. Having *fun* sounds like a good start. We're pixies, after all. "

"There's that *smell* again," Echo murmured.

Her brother nodded. "Uh-huh. Real stinky. Makes me

wanna take off my boots and knit a sweater. Now I *know* you have something specific in mind."

Z had no idea what the sweater part meant, but she laughed anyway. *They're not gonna give up until they're convinced I've told them everything.* "Okay, fine."

"Excellent." Domino nodded.

"Don't fuck it up," Echo added with a raised eyebrow.

"That envelope we pulled out of the human's deposit box." Z looked at her cousins.

The cramped office was silent, then Domino chuckled. "From our last job? That bank?"

"Yeah. The letter with the Oriceran symbols stamped on it."

Echo sighed. "All those watches we snatched are looking pretty interesting right now."

"Oh, come on." Z tossed her hands up before letting them drop on the office chair's armrests. A *snap* followed the impacts, and a small piece of plastic cracked off and toppled to the floor. "You guys aren't curious about how the hell a human got something like that?"

"Humans get all kinds of stupid crap." Domino readjusted his butt on the edge of the desk, then counted on his fingers. "Mud puddles. Trash cans. Other people's houses. Other people's *beds*. Bad hair days."

"War." Echo spread her arms above her head as if she were dancing in the sunshine instead of cooped up inside. "Famine. Plague. Murder. Taxes."

"Ooh, yeah. *Taxes*." Domino pointed at his sister. "That's a good one. Thank your little black heart that we don't ever have to deal with *those*."

"I'm guessing that's a no, then," Z interjected. All the

ridiculous things her cousins had said had gone in one ear and out the other. She'd spent her entire life perfecting selective hearing when it came to these two. "Neither of you is even a *little* curious about random humans locking away Oriceran symbols in their bank box?"

"I mean…" Domino spread his arms. "Not when we could just zip right into said bank vault and take whatever we wanted."

"We're good at that," Echo added. If she'd been anyone else, the statement would have come with a smile and sounded happy.

"And after that?" Z kicked against the floor, and the office chair rolled back, then thumped into the wall again. A screw on the underside of the seat fell out and made a gentle, metallic tinkle as it bounced across the floor. "I don't like it. Whoever owned that box, he obviously had no idea who or what he was messing with."

Domino snorted. "You sound like he did something to you personally."

"Feels like it." Z tossed a hand at the locked door. "Especially when every other human who knows we exist thinks we're a bunch of freaks who can't do anything right."

"Correction." Her cousin thrust a finger into the air and lifted his chin in a surprisingly scholarly fashion. "We *can't* do anything right, according to human standards. I'm gonna tell you right now, Z, those standards are *way* sub-par."

Echo raised her eyebrows in her version of a casual smile. "Six feet under, even."

"Funny." Z tried to keep a straight face, but it was hard

despite having spent hundreds of years listening to her cousin's morbid comments.

"Forget about the dumb envelope," Domino added, waving the topic away. "That doesn't have anything to do with anything."

Z glowered at him. "Says you."

"Yeah. Says me." He pointed at her. "You know what your problem is?"

"Oh, boy." She rolled her eyes and pretended not to be amused by her cousin's efforts to get her mind and her anger off the envelope that apparently only *she* found interesting.

"Too much color." Echo jerked her chin up and pointed at her cousin. "Too many teeth in your smile."

Z glanced at her in mock exasperation. "You know he's just gonna tell me."

The goth shrugged. "I'm just covering what he's going to leave out of his partially accurate assessment. Of you. Obvs."

"Of course." Slumping in the chair, Z waved for Domino to continue answering his rhetorical question. Everyone knew what was coming.

"*You*, Z Thornbrook of the Hollow Forest, need a job."

Z and Echo stared at him, waiting for the rest, but that was it. With a snort, Z crossed one leg over the other. "*That* was underwhelming."

"I'm serious."

"I *have* a job, Dom. We all do."

"Yeah, and they're doing *such* a great job of utilizing our skills." He held up both hands and wiggled his fingers, either referring to idle hands or saying they all had magic.

Possibly both. "I'm talking about a job *inside* a job. You feel me?"

"Mm, nope."

"Something to do. Purpose. Pleasure."

Echo interlaced her fingers and stretched them in front of her until her knuckles gave a series of cracks. "If it's the pain-inflicting kind, I'm down."

"Down, Pain Master." Domino pointed at his sister without looking away from Z. "You need something to do, right? That's what I'm hearing."

Z swept her gaze around the room. "We're stuck in an office."

"Even better!" He jumped off the desk, clapped his hands, and looked all over like he was about to start pulling ingredients off the shelves for a five-star meal. "If we're good at one thing, it's working with what we've got."

"Also, making humans cry." Echo folded her arms and tossed her hair out of her eyes. "Don't forget that part."

"Yeah, yeah. Sure. We'll figure out a way to shove it all together." Domino began a meandering perusal of the office, scanning the shelves from ceiling to floor and shoving random boxes and crates aside with the toe of his boot. "This calls for some investigative prowess."

Z laughed. "That's supposed to come from *you*?"

"Well, I figured you might wanna help, but feel free to sit on your ass while your cousins save it." He shrugged, pulled open the top left-hand drawer of the desk, and looked at Z moping in the chair. The tight, all-business line of his lips morphed into a crooked smile as he wiggled his eyebrows.

Z snorted. "You two saving *my* ass?"

"Yeah, well, a promise goes both ways. In case you forgot."

"Oh, *that's* what it means."

Domino shut the desk drawer before continuing his perusal of the random items around them. He didn't look at her again but continued his mission to find what she needed, whatever that was. Apparently, he was convinced they'd find that here.

CHAPTER FIVE

Giving her cousin the benefit of the doubt, Z let Domino search the cramped office for the thing that would "save her ass" and didn't intervene. *Maybe he needs to play the hero too. Fine by me. I can't take credit for* everything.

That made her chuckle. The copper pixie almost shot her a curious look but remembered he was trying *not* to let himself get distracted from his new purpose. Kicking aside another open cardboard box half-filled with random papers, Domino looked at his sister. "Echo, what do you think?"

The goth still hadn't moved, and she seemed bored watching her brother scurry around the small room. "I think we save her ass all the time. She just doesn't realize it."

"That's not what I asked." Domino straightened from peering under the desk and pointed at her. "But good point."

"Wow." Z folded her arms. "I appreciate the sentiment, guys. Honestly. Especially when you've found such a great way to keep yourselves busy while I sit back and wait some more."

Echo shook her head. "I have no idea what he's looking for."

"That's the point." Domino thrust a finger into the air and turned in a circle. "Nobody ever knows what they're looking for until they find it. If anybody thinks they do, they're lying to themselves. The whole point is in the aha moment. Otherwise, it's no fun. Then lightning strikes."

"I'd be down with that." Echo shrugged. "Maybe it could strike *you*."

Z giggled. "No. If he gets hit by lightning, he'll be like the Energizer Pixie times a million."

Domino kept up at the pretense of looking for a distraction worthy of his cousin's attention. "I can't, I won't, and I don't stop. I bet lightning packs a hell of a punch, though."

"Sad part is you can't punch it back."

Echo lifted her chin. "*That's* where all the fun is."

"Hey." He frowned at her. "Whose side are you on?"

"Hmm. I'm gonna say the *lightning's* side. Doesn't matter who's getting hit."

"You and your violence." Brushing it off with good-natured amusement, Domino shook his head and went back to the first drawer he'd searched. "Makes me think of those two brownies in Michigan. Remember? What were their names?"

"Dumb and Dumber?" Echo offered.

Her brother was used to ignoring her, but it was even easier for Z. She knew what Domino was trying to get at with his seemingly crazed rant. "You mean Skinny and Top?"

"That's *right*. Skinny and Top." He shot her a frown, then shook his head. "Brownies have the silliest names."

Echo spread her arms. "That's what *I* said."

"Didn't one of them swear by lightning strikes?" Domino asked. "That it made him, like, superpowered or something?"

Z raised an eyebrow. "He also swore by eating fish guts right before they helped Calinda's gang break into that antique wine cellar."

"True. True." Domino wagged a finger. "Still, the way he talked about it almost made me wanna try—"

A loud trill ripped through the office, stunning them into confused silence. Z sat up in her chair, trying to place the source. Domino hastily looked around, then scratched his head.

When the noise rose again, the pixies realized it was coming from the old clunky phone beside the old clunky desktop computer on the desk.

They grimaced in distaste as they stared at the phone and the red light blinking beneath the button labeled Line 1.

Domino took a step away from the desk. "I thought the sound of Major Winters' super-fun lectures was bad."

Z kicked the scuffed linoleum floor with the heel of her boot, rolling the chair farther away. "With all their fancy tech, you'd think at least humans would be smart enough to put sounds in telephones that don't make your ears bleed."

Echo glared at the device. "Makes me wanna gouge somebody's eyes out."

The office was silent. Then the obnoxious trill rang out again.

Echo rolled her eyes and stalked toward the desk. "I'll take care of it."

"Whoa, whoa. Hold your seahorses." Domino raised a hand to stop her, ignoring the apathetic stare he got in return. "We were *just* talking about Z needing something to do."

"You're right." Echo raised an eyebrow at Z. "I'll give you three seconds to blast that thing to smithereens. Any longer, and I'll take over."

With a snort of disbelief, Domino turned to face Z and gestured at the telephone. "You wanted a job, right?"

Z wrinkled her nose.

"And we're stuck in here for however long the boss says to stay. *Right?*"

When Z looked at him, Domino flashed his signature grin and wiggled his eyebrows at her. "You want me to play Army secretary?"

"Oh, come on. I don't think you've ever tried something and not been, like—" He jolted and grimaced at the next ring. "Been the best at it right away. Here you go, Z. Here's your new job calling you. Literally."

She almost burst out laughing, but Domino looked serious. Echo didn't look like she cared, but when the phone rang again, Z sighed and gave in. "Fine."

"Fine?"

"Yeah, fine. I'll give it a shot." She rolled the office chair back to the desk, then paused her hand hovering above the phone as she waited for the headache-inducing sound to return.

When it did, Z snatched the handpiece from its cradle and lifted it to her ear. "US Army Boring Division. How may I ruin your day?"

The silence on the other end of the line lasted far longer than she'd expected, and she looked questioningly at Domino. Her cousin kept grinning and gave her two thumbs-up.

The person who had dialed the number cleared his throat and responded. "Uh, look. Just put Packard on."

"Oh, *I'm* sorry." Doing her best impersonation of someone who cared, Z thumped her elbow on the desk and cocked her head to keep the phone pressed against her ear. "Packard isn't in right now."

To make sure, Echo looked over her shoulder at the closed and locked office door.

The caller sighed and cleared his throat. "And?"

"And he's still not here?" Z plastered a sweet smile on her face and batted her eyelashes, which made her end of the conversation feel more fun since whoever was in a hurry to speak to Packard couldn't see her.

"Huh. I don't see any requests for personal leave."

"Oh, no," Z corrected. "I don't think he ever wants to go home."

"Well, is he sick or something?"

"No, he's feeling *great*! Volunteered to take the poodles out for their weekly grooming and everything." Now that she had a job, it was much easier to forget how frustrated she'd been a few minutes ago. Being a pixie and doing what pixies did best was the best way to turn a bad day around.

Grinning, she continued her spiel before the caller could even *try* to puzzle out what she'd just said. "If you'd like to leave a message, I'll be happy to pass it along when he's finished with his massage."

The person on the other end was deathly silent, which made Domino's and Echo's supportive snickering sound that much louder. The man looking for Packard let out a confused grunt and muttered, "The fuck?"

Z held up one finger in a mocking request for silence. "Oh, dear. There must be something wrong with our connection."

"I'm not in the mood for jokes. Put Packard on the line."

"He would *never* joke about the poodles," Z replied sweetly. For good measure, she added, "Sir."

"Goddammit." Before Z could think of something else witty and annoying enough to get under the man's skin, there was a sharp click in her ear, and the line went dead.

"Hello? *Hello?*" She held the phone away, looked at it in confusion, and set it down on its cradle with a shrug. "Guess it wasn't important enough to leave a name and a callback number."

"Hey, if he can't stay focused enough to figure out what he wants, that's *his* problem." Domino clapped a hand on his cousin's shoulder and gave it a shake. "*You* were brilliant."

Z batted her eyelashes at him and spoke in her happy-go-lucky receptionist's voice. "You think so?"

"Killed it," Echo stated.

Z and Domino burst out laughing, and the copper pixie pointed at the phone. "I can tell you this. Packard would be *lucky* to have you taking all his calls."

With a smirk, she scanned the surface of the desk. Her gaze landed on the computer monitor she hadn't paid any attention to until this moment. The screen clicked on with a bright flash of light that faded to a backlit blue. "What about handling his emails?"

"Huh?"

While her cousin rounded the edge of the desk to get a good look at the screen, Z grabbed the mouse and started clicking, her eyes widening with excitement. "Scheduling meetings. Fixing his calendar. Ooh! Look at *this*. Somebody has to go pick up the major's *dry cleaning*."

"Whew." Domino sighed and shook his head, then gazed at his cousin in adoration. "He doesn't deserve you."

"I know. You think it's time to ask for a raise?"

He leaned over the desk for a closer look at the items on Packard's personal computer, which were laid out on the screen for everyone to see. "I mean, he *did* leave himself signed into the system."

"Yeah, you're right." Z sniffed and opened the sergeant's calendar for a more thorough perusal of today's priority to-dos. "Too soon to ask for a raise. I'll just have to keep proving my worth."

"Now you're talking."

On the other side of the desk, Echo let out an enormous yawn and patted her mouth. The next second, she returned to her natural size and zipped across the office in a streak of silver light. Settling on top of the monitor, her Army OCP uniform black from collar to boots, she set the screen into a violent wobble.

"Whoa." Z shot out a hand to stabilize the monitor, then fixed her cousin with a disapproving scowl. "If I didn't know better, I'd say you're trying to cut this short before we even get to the good part."

"And I'd say you're enjoying yourself," the goth shot back.

Domino snapped his fingers and pointed at his sister. "If you're not gonna add something productive, go sit down."

He didn't expect his sister to comply, so he wasn't surprised when she jumped straight up and slammed her tiny form back down onto the monitor. Then she sat down like the plastic frame was a park bench.

Z chuckled. "Look who'd make a great paperweight."

Echo started kicking her feet, systematically slamming the heel of each boot against the screen. The impacts sent a ripple of distorted light away from the place the boots landed. Her cousin and her brother tried to ignore her temper tantrum.

"Hey, look at this." Z pointed with the mouse, still holding the monitor to keep Echo from knocking it over. "Packard's got some important meetings to get to. With a major and a lieutenant colonel. Ooh, and a five-star general."

Domino stroked his chin and squinted at the screen. "Yeah, but where's the general with five *fingers*? That's what *I* wanna know."

"I bet we could sniff him out if we click around enough." She explored a bit longer, then sighed. "Calendars are stupid. There's not enough room to see everything at once since you gotta go into every single day to see beginning to end."

"There's gotta be a way to make the writing smaller,"

Domino suggested helpfully. "Or the typing. Or whatever makes those little letters. To get it all to fit in one place, right?"

Echo just kept pounding her tiny combat boots' heels on the screen as she watched her cousin and her brother with total boredom. Anyone who knew pixies and their moods would have been able to tell things were about to get a lot louder and more chaotic.

For the pixies present, it meant things were about to get exciting. For the next little while, at least.

"Nah." Z started clicking on Packard's digital calendar. "There's only one way to get all this neat and tidy again. Then we can build everything again from scratch the *right* way."

"Ah."

"Seriously, I don't know *how* he's been keeping all this straight for as long as he has."

Domino shook his head in mock pity. "Poor man. They should've stuck us in here sooner."

"Tell me about it." Z had just highlighted every entry on the sergeant's calendar when Echo made an impatient sound and zipped off the monitor. She darted past Z's face, but the blue-haired pixie was so intent on her work that she didn't even flinch.

Neither Z nor Domino paid Echo any attention when she thumped into the closest stack of binders on the back wall shelves and disappeared.

"*Oh*, yeah." Z clicked and dragged and clicked and dragged. "This is just the kind of makeover he needed."

Domino snorted as he watched over her shoulder. "Talk about a faulty system. Oh, hey. What's that?"

"Huh. Delete All."

He smirked. "More like Fresh Start."

"Great minds, Dom. Great minds."

Two seconds later, every item on Packard's calendar was swirling down the figurative drain. The pixies broke into excited giggles.

"Aw, look at it go!"

"Cutest trashcan I've ever seen."

"It *dances*."

"Yeah, you're a *happy* little computer trashcan, aren't you? Happy *and* hungry. Yes, you were. Yes, you were."

While Domino made baby faces at the ancient version of the computer's recycle bin, Z sat back and looked for something else to do. Her smile faded because even after a job well done, she didn't feel satisfied.

"I don't know, Dom. It's missing something."

"What? You mean you didn't *like* giving him a brand-new start? A clean slate? Fresh undies?"

She folded her arms and quirked her lips in consideration. "Trust me; I like it. But all this? I mean, what's the point of helping Packard straighten out his abysmal secretarial skills if we don't show him how to *improve*? It feels...unfinished."

Domino shrugged. "So we refill his calendar. Send a few emails. Schedule more meetings. But, like, ones that matter. Oh! We should make *templates*."

"Well, shit." Z snapped her fingers, then clapped her cousin's arm. "I don't care what anybody says about your Army tests, Dom. You're a genius in my book."

"That's the only book I ever care about." He straightened, puffed out his chest, and put his hands on his hips. "Thanks."

"So, how do we fill all this empty space with stuff that matters?"

"It's gotta be something good. Something he *deserves*."

Z echoed her cousin's contemplative pose and stroked her chin in thought. "Too bad nobody thought it would be important to give three new magical recruits all the pertinent information on Army personnel."

Domino shook his head. "A real shame. You don't think they keep a list around, do you? Like, names and ranks and where these bigwigs are and how to find them in the system or—"

A silver streak darted past their heads to the desk. Domino didn't get a chance to complete his musings because the loud thump of something very heavy and very solid landing made him and Z both look for the source.

The three-ring binder was four inches thick and stuffed to bursting with a daunting number of papers. It wasn't, however, the size of the binder or the sight of Echo standing beside it with her arms folded and one bite-sized combat boot tapping in impatience that caught Z's and Domino's attention. It was the title of the binder, which appeared to have been penned in Packard's own hand.

Z stared at it. "*Master Contact List, 307th Combat Battalion, Special Operations*. Well, isn't *that* convenient?"

"Plus *Annual Events and Appearances*," Domino added as he pointed at the subtitle written neatly beneath the first line. "Don't wanna leave any of *that* out."

"No, of course not."

They both turned their heads to Echo, who still looked bored and ready to start serious trouble.

"Echo," Z said, "smiley faces or no smiley faces, you're a genius too."

The goth just raised her eyebrows. "I know."

"Why would Packard keep a list of all this stuff *on paper*?" Domino asked with both amusement and mischief in his voice.

"Huh." Z pretended to think about it. "I'm guessing he doesn't trust computers. Or technology. Might not even trust *himself* to remember who's who and what's what if he doesn't write it down."

"That's a hell of a lot of extra work."

"He doesn't trust *us*, either," Echo added.

"Well, that was his first mistake." Domino pointed at the huge binder, and copper light burst from his fingertip and hit the white plastic with a jolting buzz. It slid across the desk so he could open it. Then they could see Packard's secrets.

Domino snickered and shook his head. "Who am I kidding? He's made *so* many mistakes."

Z grabbed the mouse and held it at the ready. "Let's give him a reason to get back on our good side."

The cramped room filled with raucous laughter, but there was no one in the labyrinthine hallways to hear it.

CHAPTER SIX

Z grinned as she saved the latest addition to the sergeant's calendar—a weekly reoccurring reminder to take the poodles out for their grooming session before stopping at the nearest spa for his massage. "There. Now nobody can say he's a hypocrite or a liar."

Domino burst out laughing. "Gotta stay honest, right? 'Cause you know somebody's gonna ask about those poodles eventually. Hey! Should we get him some actual poodles?"

"Hmm. That *would* make it so much more believable. Where do poodles come from?"

"You can look up anything on the internet," Echo suggested from the top of the computer monitor. She'd turned the strip of protective plastic into something of a bed and now lay there overseeing the entire project.

"Internet." Z rolled the word around on her tongue and pursed her lips. "You know, that word always makes me feel itchy."

"And what does it *catch*?" Domino added. "Besides poodles, obviously."

Echo reached her tiny hands up into the air above her and counted on her fingers. "How to hide a dead body. Where to buy the sharpest butcher knives. Best ways to poison a human without them knowing it."

"Ha!" Z stared at her cousin in disbelief. "When did you have the time to figure out how to cast the internet?"

"Marv showed me."

"Good ol' Marv." Domino swung a fist in front of himself in nostalgic approval of their former crewmates. "Hope those guys are doing okay."

"They're fine." Z nodded firmly. She and her cousins tried not to dwell on the fact that Calinda's entire gang had been returned to Oriceran without them, but she knew in her bones that it was true. "They've probably started some kinda new regime over there by now."

"Could've started one here if they'd stayed," Echo murmured. "After getting rid of all the humans, obviously."

The office fell silent, then Z shrugged and pulled the keyboard toward her again. "Okay. So what do I type in here? 'How to catch poodles on the internet?'"

"Sounds about right." Folding his arms, Domino leaned back. Where gravity and physics would have come into play for anyone else and dropped them straight to the ground, his copper wings fluttered, holding him in place. He looked like he was in an invisible hammock. "Hey, what do those things eat, anyway?"

Z snorted and shook her head as she typed away. "You make friends with literally every critter we meet, Dom. But you don't know what poodles eat?"

"You're missing one major piece of that puzzle. Critters are critters. They're wild. They live in trees or underground. Sometimes in dumpsters, but hey, who am I to judge?" The toes of his boots dipped up and down mid-air as he considered the differences. "But poodles are, like, *domesticated*."

He whispered the last word, and he and Z shivered with disgust and horror. Even Echo groaned from her place atop the monitor. "Another reason to punch humans' faces in."

"You'd think that, right?" Domino shook his head and sighed. "I had a hard time buying it too when I heard how it works out for both of them. They *like* it."

"Of course they do," Z replied distractedly, clicking around the search engine, looking for Packard's new poodles. "Humans think everything they do is the best thing anyone's ever done."

"No, I mean the poodles."

"Oh." She paused, then fixed her cousin with a disbelieving frown. "They *like* it?"

"I mean, the chihuahua I talked to one time seemed pretty adamant about it. Then again, he couldn't tell me *why* he thought it was such a good deal, but I had to take his word for it."

"Damn. Look at this." Z gestured toward the computer screen. "Three thousand dollars for a poodle. And we have to get him *two*. How much do you guys have?"

"On me?" The copper pixie patted down his uniform pockets. "Zilch. Would've had a lot more if that gnome and Alpha Team hadn't blasted it all out of existence when they blew our treehouse apart."

"But then we wouldn't have gotten to fight back." Echo let out a wistful sigh. "So worth it."

"Then I guess we need to find out how much Packard has on him. He needs these poodles."

The pixies shared a look of renewed dedication, then all three of them burst into action. Z and Domino popped into their pixie sizes to join Echo in zipping back and forth around the office.

Drawers were hauled open and out of the desk and let topple to the floor. Cardboard boxes and plastic storage totes scooted back and forth as the pixies systematically rooted and sifted through them. Loose papers fluttered all over the office as the pixies studied everything that belonged to Packard as well as everything that didn't.

"What kinda person doesn't keep their money with the rest of their important stuff?" Z asked, tossing two more plastic-wrapped packages out of one box and over her shoulder without bothering to see what they were.

"I bet he just made a list of everything he has," Domino added. "He's a dummy, but he's a thorough dummy. I'll give him that."

"What about this?" Echo zipped off the top of another bookshelf holding a medium-sized hinged box above her head. The box's exterior had been painted jet-black and lacquered to a pristine shine. It hovered above her as if she held a tiny loaf of bread instead of a well-crafted piece of woodwork five times her size.

"Yeah. Okay." Domino snorted. "You *would* pick the black box."

She didn't wait for any further response before flicking open the box's lid and upending it. She spilled its contents all over the floor, shaking it with both hands. One metallic clang after another echoed through the tiny office. "Jackpot."

"Seriously?" Z poked her head up.

"Yes!" Domino thrust both open hands into the air, then dove to the floor where the box's contents were still spinning on the linoleum. "Look at that! You picked the right box!"

"What was in it?" Z asked.

"Coins." Domino dropped to the ground and lifted the first metal coin. It was too large for spare change. "Damn. You ever seen one of these before?"

"We *stole* money, Dom." Z joined her cousin in perusing the coins all over the floor. "Can't say any of us ever took the time to *study* it."

"Well, it's definitely a coin. They all are. What does this one say?" He squinted and held the coin as far away from his face as possible, which was fairly difficult, seeing as it was almost the same size as he was. "'Commander's Excellence'? What the heck is that?"

"Maybe it's, like, really old or something." With a shrug, Z picked up another coin, this one a nice, shiny silver. "Says, 'Mission Accomplished.' Huh. Does money normally have Army stuff written on it?"

"Oh, shit. It's *Army* money!"

Echo tossed the black box across the office, then joined the other pixies examining the coins on the floor. The first one she picked up went right to her mouth, and she bit down on it with a quick crunch and clang before dropping the whole thing right there at her feet. "Tastes like shit."

Z kicked another one aside. "What the hell made you wanna eat it?"

The goth shrugged. "Saw a pirate do it once. He'd probably say it tastes like shit too."

"Damnit, those poodles aren't *in* the Army." Domino dropped the coin he was holding with a sigh of frustration. The coin bounced once off the linoleum, spun through the air, and barely missed clipping the top of Z's shoulder as it went. "These things are useless."

"Humans are so confusing." Echo kicked at another coin and shook her head. "Why would they make a bunch of money they can't even use?"

"You know what?" Z stuck her hands on her hips and surveyed the highly disappointing mess of overlarge military coins. "The whole Army would do a lot better for themselves if they stopped focusing on the confusing stuff and came up with a use for everything. Like figuring out what they're good at. What their strengths are. Besides wasting our time, obviously."

"Hey, that's a good idea." Domino pointed at her. "We could make a list. Lay out all the things the Army does right there for them to see, and we could, like, replace it all with way more useful stuff. I don't think making giant-ass coins with mysterious sayings is gonna make it on the 'How To Be Better' list, though."

"Yeah, they suck at this." After kicking aside yet another coin, Z darted into the air to get a better aerial view of what they *hadn't* yet searched in the cramped office. "Keep looking. We're bound to find *something* valuable in here."

"Like this?" Echo now hovered at the highest shelf. She grabbed the top layer of stuff from the shelf and tossed it over her shoulder, letting it land with a hollow smack. A second and third object followed, then a steady stream of items rained down on top of her brother.

Domino avoided every projectile, then picked one up and wrinkled his nose. "It's plastic."

"Plastic what?" Z asked.

"I don't know. Just a plastic card. With...oh, *hey*. I thought Sergeant Packard's first name was Sergeant. But look." He turned the large plastic card over—this one a bright red—so the outside faced his cousin and trailed a finger under the raised and bumpy words printed there. "This says James L. Packard. Not sure what the L stands for. Didn't he used to be a corporal? He apparently got a promotion."

"Loser," Echo murmured before flinging the rest of the plastic cards around the room. "Leotard. Lime. Lichen."

"Ooh. Lichen. I like that."

Z didn't bother to correct Domino in that he'd gestured toward the name on the card from right to left instead of in the correct direction. Wrinkling her nose, she found herself more interested in why the sergeant would keep so much useless junk around him at all times. "Why'd he put his name on them?"

"I don't know. Guess he's a big fan of himself." With a snort, Domino tossed the card aside, and the pixies kept looking.

As wrapped up as Z and her cousins were in their diligent work to find the funds for the poodles to back up Sergeant Packard's new schedule, updated calendar items, improved contact list, and priority to-dos, they weren't too caught up to be aware of the sharp clip of footsteps growing louder in the hall.

"Wait, wait. Shh." Z froze and cocked her head. "That's definitely somebody coming our way."

Domino popped his head up over the top of a desk drawer sending out a flurry of loose papers, rubber bands, and a paperclip. "Who?"

"I don't have x-ray vision, Dom."

"Yeah, but you *could*."

"Great." Echo heaved a sigh. "Probably more *tests*."

The pixies probably wouldn't have cared if the person so diligently heading down the hall hadn't received a call and chosen to answer it. "This is Sergeant Packard."

"No *way*," Domino whispered. "What are the odds?"

"I'm heading there right now, sir," Packard continued, his voice growing closer and louder. "No, sir. It's fine. I mean… Well, it's not what *I* would've picked, but that's not my job. Yes, sir. I'll keep you updated."

"Shit." Z let out a squeak when Packard's keys jingled in the hallway close to the door.

"Nobody told us we were waiting for *him* in his office," Domino murmured. "It's gonna ruin the surprise."

"We could kidnap him," Echo suggested. "Tie him up. Throw him in a closet somewhere. Then he'd never know."

"Yeah, neither would anyone else."

The goth fixed Z with a deadpan stare. "That's the point."

The footsteps stopped, and the keys jingled again. Finally, a single key slid into the lock, and the doorknob started to turn.

As seriously as he took his job and all the duties that

came with being assigned to work under Major Winters, Sergeant Packard hadn't been happy to hear the three new recruits had been shoved into *his* office to kill the last few hours. He was more unhappy when he opened the door.

When he peered inside, he saw the opposite of what he'd expected to find.

All three pixies stood at their full human sizes in the center of the room, their OCP uniforms making them look like they belonged there. If it hadn't been for the goth's against-regulation blacks and the three sets of gossamer wings protruding from their backs, Packard would have thought these three were like every other regular soldier he'd encountered.

As he stared at them, he found himself fervently missing those banal, boring, benign everyday interactions with banal, boring, benign, *normal* Army soldiers. These definitely weren't them, and Sergeant Packard was even more unsettled by the fact everything seemed perfectly normal. That was, of course, as long as he ignored the fact two of them were whistling aimless tunes with their hands clasped behind their backs while the third casually picked nonexistent dirt out from under her fingernails.

Yeah right. Nothing *about this is even a little suspicious...*

The sergeant gave himself a few more seconds to scan his temporary office, then scrutinized the pixies' casual stances and the fact that none of them had so much as looked at him yet.

"What are you doing?" he asked and immediately wished he hadn't. He'd wanted his words to come across as skeptical and authoritative, but the question sounded more like an annoying little sibling asking what the big kids were doing because he wanted in on the fun.

It got the pixies' attention, though.

Z whipped her head toward Packard and widened her eyes. "Oh, *hi*, Sergeant. Didn't hear you come in."

Domino feigned surprise with as much over-reactive enthusiasm as Z. "Wow. Look at you. You've really been working on your stealth game, huh?"

Echo kept picking at her nails.

Sergeant Packard's frown deepened as he scanned his office again. Not a single thing looked out of place, messed with, or like it was about to either explode or fall apart at a second's notice. That didn't get rid of the feeling that he'd just missed something incredibly important. He cleared his throat and managed this time to sound much more like a prying parent than an annoying little sibling, which was only marginally better. "What did you touch?"

"Us?" Z set a hand on her own chest as if there were a dozen other soldiers in the room with her.

Echo finally stopped picking her nails to look at him. The slow way she folded her arms and fixed him with her deadpan stare didn't quite carry the level of respect and attentiveness his rank was generally afforded.

Domino clicked his tongue. "So it's like that, huh, Sergeant?"

"Like what?"

"We haven't seen you all day, and you storm in here like the place is on fire, and the only thing on your mind is whether we *touched* anything? Not even so much as a 'hello' first." The copper pixie fixed his NCO with a disapproving frown and tsked again as he shook his head. "Not a great way to boost soldier morale around here, know what I'm saying?"

"What?" Packard wrinkled his nose and couldn't reconcile the fact he *knew* these pixies had been up to something—because they always were—with the complete lack of proof in front of him. Everything seemed perfectly fine and normal. "Morale has nothing to do with it."

"Ouch." Domino recoiled like he'd been slapped, then pretended to pout and rubbed his chest right over his heart. "We *all* have feelings, Sergeant."

"Yeah, and I have a feeling you three lunatics are hiding something. So I'll ask you one more time. What did you touch?"

The pixies shared a quick glance, the kind that made Packard certain that they could read each other's minds and made the hairs rise on the back of his neck. Domino grinned and lifted both hands in concession, showing they were empty. Unfortunately, that only meant Packard hadn't found the problem yet. "Nothing, Sergeant."

"Not a thing." Z lifted her hands, copying her cousin's conceding stance. "See?"

"Honest."

When the sergeant's gaze darted toward Echo, he found the goth still staring at him with her arms folded. She didn't offer a single word or even a gesture that was supposed to hint at innocence.

I'm not screwing around with that one ever again. Should've requested a transfer the day she touched my face.

Scowling even more deeply, the man took as much time as he dared for another visual sweep of his office and found everything in its place. For now. Only then did he realize he still held the outer edge of the door in a tense, anxious grip. He stepped back into the hallway and opened the door all the way. "Congratulations. You managed not to screw something up. Let's go."

"Ooh, goodie." Domino clapped his hands and bounced up and down on his heels. "A trip with Sergeant Packard."

"Where are you taking us this time?" Z asked as she stepped nimbly across the perfectly clean floor.

The sergeant had to release the door as she made it into the hallway since he couldn't step as far enough away from her as he wanted while still holding onto it.

"Is it ice cream?" Domino asked with a juvenile grin. "I bet it's ice cream."

"That's so *nice* of you, Sergeant."

"Hey, Echo. You hear that? Sergeant Packard's taking us out for ice cream!"

Standing just outside his office, Packard couldn't help but stare at the all-black pixie bringing up the rear as the last to finally step out of his office. Echo stopped in front of him, her expression unchanging and unreadable, and thrust her open palm toward him like she expected him to drop a pint and three spoons into it right then and there.

"No." He glanced quickly between Echo's blank mask and the open office door, but when she clearly didn't plan on moving out of the way for him, he skirted quickly around her to grab the door and slam it shut. "I never said anything about ice cream."

"*Now* you tell us." Domino tossed his hands up.

"You feeling okay, Sergeant?" Z asked as the pixies waited for their NCO to finish locking up his office again so he could lead the way. "You're not your usual self today."

"I'm fine." Packard ripped the key out of the doorknob, thrust the keyring into his pants pocket, and headed swiftly down the hall, all while trying not to look like his proximity to the recruits was making him jumpy. "And if I wasn't, I sure as hell wouldn't talk to any of *you* about it."

"Aw, how come?"

"We're great listeners, Sergeant."

"Maybe all you need is a fresh perspective."

"Hey, yeah. You know who's *really* good at that?"

"Echo."

"Echo. Trust me. If you think whatever you're going through is bad, now, she'll make it a piece of cake. My sister can turn anything into its own worst nightmare!"

Domino and Z snickered, and Sergeant Packard picked up the pace, his fists clenched at his sides, a sheen of sweat forming on his forehead.

I hate these morons. So much. And I don't hate people.

He couldn't bring himself to say anything to their obvious attempts to goad him into a reaction since they would only use it against him. He'd learned his lesson the first time he'd been left alone with the OIP's flagship magical recruits.

Do your job, Packard. Just do your job, and then this'll all be over.

Repeating that over and over as he led the pixies through the halls was the only thing that made it possible for him to drown out the sound of their provoking jokes and ribald laughter along the way.

CHAPTER SEVEN

After so much time spent cooped up, Z and her cousins took it for granted that they were being led to yet another room.

The pixies had spent several weeks performing private nighttime expeditions through the disorienting maze, and just because Major Winters had returned their personal effects after Bootcamp didn't mean they'd forgotten those journeys.

They knew this part of the facility like the backs of their hands. They'd just given up paying attention to where they were going since being led from one room to the next for one useless test or bout of more waiting had become their new normal.

When Sergeant Packard stopped his brisk march down the hall, Z didn't notice they were in a new part of the facility until she heard a ding and the sound of elevator doors sliding open instead of the usual squeak of a twisting doorknob. Her cousins picked it up just as quickly, and they all stared at the elevator.

"This is it," Domino murmured.

Z leaned toward her cousin. "We don't know that yet."

"I can feel it." He looked like he was about to explode with excitement but managed to keep it relatively under control.

Packard stepped briskly into the elevator first and waited for the pixies to join him. Domino took up the rear, and once he'd stepped inside after everyone else, he spun smartly to face the closing elevator doors before he just couldn't hold it in any longer. "This is it! Right, Sergeant?"

"I have no idea what you're talking about, but probably not." With a quick eye roll, Packard tried to reach through Echo and Domino standing in front of him so he could touch the control panel. It had been a mistake to step into such a small elevator before everyone else, and he leaned forward in the hopes of subtly reaching the buttons.

Echo shot him a warning look and made a sound he'd never expected to hear from any soldier, let alone one who'd been blatantly allowed to walk around in all-black OCPs.

Holy shit. Is she growling at me?

He instantly dropped his hand to his side and cleared his throat.

"The moment we've been waiting for," Domino continued delightedly, rocking back and forth on his heels. "Come on, Sergeant. You can tell us."

"I have no idea what you're talking about," Packard murmured. "Press the button for G1, would you?"

"The button?" Domino looked over his shoulder at the sergeant with a confused frown. "Oh, the *elevator* button."

He nudged his sister's shoulder and whispered, "Press the button."

Echo sighed but didn't move to do what she'd been told.

"G1, huh?" Domino rocked on his heels again. "I knew it."

"I'm not trying to stand in this elevator all day," Packard muttered through clenched teeth. "So let's get a move on."

"The sergeant's looking paler than usual, Echo," Z added as she looked Packard up and down. "You're gonna give him a heart attack if you don't press the button."

Echo clicked her tongue, then leaned toward Domino to whisper in his ear.

Her brother choked out a laugh, then looked over his shoulder at Packard one more time before shaking his head. "You don't mean that."

The goth shrugged but continued to stand in front of the closed elevator doors without pushing the button to take them to G1.

"Maybe you just need some fresh air," Z said as she leaned slightly toward Packard and lowered her voice. "I knew this Willen once who couldn't *stand* small spaces. You know, the cramped ones where it feels like the walls are closing in on you and there's no room to breathe. What's that called?"

"Clusterfuckish," Domino replied confidently, then he paused, cocked his head, and wrinkled his nose. "Wait. Clamsterphobe. Clamorphonic. Shit, you know what I mean."

"I'm fine," Packard snapped, then he cleared his throat, tugged at the top button of his uniform shirt, and tried to act as if escorting pixies was something he'd done every day for years.

Secretly, he thought it was something he'd never get used to. It definitely didn't help that his uniform was damp with sweat. "Just press the damn—"

Echo pointed at the elevator's control panel and shot a quick dart of silver light at the button labeled G1. Her magic crackled and fizzled against the button with a loud pop.

Sergeant Packard shoved himself back against the rear wall of the elevator.

Z looked him up and down. "It's totally harmless, you know. Our magic."

Packard didn't say a word.

"Yeah, totally," Domino agreed, though he was more distracted that the elevator hadn't started moving yet. "Unless we want it to be *un*-harmless. Obviously."

"Jesus Christ," Packard whispered. "What's wrong with using your finger?"

Domino snickered. "Hear that? He wants you to give him the finger."

Echo raised her eyebrows, then lifted her hand toward her shoulder, fully intending to grace Sergeant Packard with the aforementioned finger before her brother smacked her hand back down.

"No, no. You gotta do it like this. The whole thing." Domino leaned forward, extended a hand toward the elevator's button panel, and proceeded to drag his hand down the entire panel from top to bottom.

"No, wait. Oh, *come on*," Sergeant Packard wailed.

"See?" Domino then dragged his hand from bottom to

top along the buttons and then again from side to side. "Like this. Hey, look. They're all lit up! Whew." He playfully nudged his sister with an elbow and chuckled. "Turns out you *didn't* break it."

"Why?" Packard spread his arms as far as the small elevator would allow when it was packed to capacity with three pixies and himself.

The elevator lurched slightly, and all three pixies giggled at the sensation of their stomachs dropping as they started to ascend.

"Why would you do that?" The sergeant huffed. "Like… what…made you think that was a good idea?"

Domino looked back at the man. "I'm just being thorough, Sergeant. That's what this whole thing is about, right?"

"No, it's an elevator."

The copper pixie giggled. "I meant the *Army*, silly. Gotta cross all the I's and dot all the T's and make sure every button lights up every time, right?"

"Besides," Z added, "you don't know when the last time somebody checked this elevator was. What if one of the buttons needed a few repairs?"

"That's not your job. That's for Maintenance," Packard said.

"Yeah, but Maintenance can't be everywhere at once," Domino replied. "That's impossible." The elevator stopped, its doors opened into yet another empty hallway, and nobody moved. "And if anyone knows what's impossible, it's us. Trust me."

"I don't," Packard muttered. "Not at all."

The elevator doors closed again, and it started to rise one more time.

"Can't hurt to make sure everything works the way it's supposed to, right?" Z waited a moment for the sergeant to offer a response, then leaned slightly forward to try to catch his attention. "Sergeant? You there?"

"He didn't get off at the last stop, did he?" Domino spun as much as the cramped space would allow, then grinned. "Oh, *there* you are. Whew."

"I know you said you're fine," Z continued, her smile fading, "but the way you're sweating and gritting your teeth right now kinda says otherwise."

"Oh, no." Domino's eyes widened. "You should've said something, Sergeant. We totally could've made a pitstop for you before cramming into this floating box."

"Shut up!" Packard shouted, and the pixies instantly complied, but now that he'd popped his top, he just couldn't keep it in any longer. "Both of you just shut up! I told you to press *one* fucking button. That's it! And you couldn't even do *that* right!"

Domino fixed the NCO with a condescending frown. "Aw, you're still on the button?"

"That was *forever* ago, Sergeant," Z added as the elevator stopped on the next floor. "Right now, we're more concerned about the state of your—"

"I don't give a fuck about what concerns you," Packard shouted at the top of his lungs, "and I don't have to take a shit!"

Just as he finished his explosive outburst, the elevator doors finished opening all the way.

It was just his luck that this particular floor happened

to have other active military personnel on it, three of whom were standing in the hallway, waiting for the elevator.

All three of them stared at the young, sweaty, red-faced sergeant surrounded by what looked like three regular soldiers. None of them were curious enough to look closely enough at the elevator's other occupants to notice the three sets of different-colored wings.

Noticing every single member of the Army was a higher rank than they were, all three of them stood to attention and saluted crisply. Stunned but used to the standard procedure, the men returned the salute.

Domino shot the men two thumbs-up and grinned, which made him look insane in comparison to his sister, who didn't move a muscle as she stared down every single one of them. Z leaned slightly to the side to peer between her cousins and offered the waiting men a wave. "Don't mind us. Just another day in the life, am I right?"

"Are...are you guys waiting for *this* elevator?" Domino asked.

The men blinked, then one of them lifted both hands in concession and said matter-of-factly, "We'll wait."

The elevator doors started to close again, and Z nodded. "Yeah, we're all *really* good at that, huh? Good luck."

"Have a great day." Domino's voice echoed down the hallway just as the doors shut, and then they were off.

The elevator was silent except for the sound of Sergeant Packard's heavy breathing and grinding teeth. Domino sucked in a breath and asked, "Any idea who those guys were?"

"Never seen 'em before." Z casually shook her head. "They seem pretty nice, though."

"Yeah, you know, they really did. You should take us on elevator rides more often, Sergeant. We can make new friends."

"No." Packard stared straight ahead at the back of Echo's motionless head.

"Everybody could use a few friends, Sergeant," Z added cheerily. "Even you."

"No."

Domino clicked his tongue. "Well, that's your loss, then, isn't it?"

The elevator stopped again, the doors opened onto yet another empty hallway, and the copper pixie rocked on his heels again while they waited. "What about, like, a field trip—"

"Shut the fuck up."

"Yeesh." The pixie rolled his eyes, then dropped his gaze toward his sister. "*Somebody's* in a mood today."

"We're just trying to help, Sergeant," Z added. "I hope you see that one day because if you keep pushing everyone away like this, nobody's gonna want to help you."

"Don't worry about it, Z. We'll grow on him. We grow on everybody."

"Like fucking parasites," Packard muttered under his breath. He realized he'd said it out loud and swallowed hard. He forced himself not to say another word on their way to G1, not even when the pixies gave contented sighs.

For the rest of their unnecessarily long elevator ride, they let him stew in his discomfort and didn't make him say another word.

CHAPTER EIGHT

G1 turned out to be just as empty and boring and bland as the other levels Z and her cousins had seen. Once they stepped out of the elevator for a quick look around, Domino's shoulders and copper wings sagged. "I really thought this was it."

"Definitely not the top floor." Z clapped a reassuring hand on his shoulder as she caught up to him. "Unless that elevator goes all the way to other levels *above* the top of the mountain."

"Oh, man. Now *that* would be awesome. Hey, Sergeant. Does the Army build skyscrapers and, like, space buildings and stuff?"

Segreant Packard stormed past them without a word and headed briskly down the hall.

Domino cocked his head. "Was I mumbling?"

"One-track mind right there," Z assessed as she and her cousins watched Packard storm away. "Looks like he's had a rough day so far."

"Wait 'til he finds our surprise." Domino wiggled his

eyebrows and shot her a sidelong glance. "That'll cheer him up."

"For sure. Come on." She led the way after the sergeant.

The only thing Sergeant Packard cared about was putting distance between him and the three magical terrors who'd turned his life upside-down.

The pixies scanned every door they passed, occasionally shrinking to dart toward the slit of a window in a door too high for humans to look through. It was also easier to catch up to Sergeant Packard. Several times, they had to dart down the hallway with more effort than expected so they didn't lose the NCO around the next corner or up a short flight of stairs.

Packard picked up on something fishy going on behind him, but every time he paused to look over his shoulder, the three of them were fifteen paces behind him, walking swiftly and confidently at human size.

With wings, he thought as he shook his head and rounded the final corner. *Wings! I can't even...*

He couldn't even finish his thought, but he'd finally come to the door where Major Winters had ordered him to leave them.

He's the one who should be doing this right now. They listen to him *as much as they listen to anyone.*

Packard's good little soldiers, intent on doing what was required of them, knocked. Then Packard twisted the knob, shoved open the door, and stepped aside, pointing the way.

"For us?" Domino's lips formed an O. "After all the trouble you just went through, Sergeant, I can't *wait* to see what happens next."

"Okay, lay it on me straight, Sergeant." Z stopped in front of him and nodded curtly. "We're finally getting out of here, right?"

"I fucking hope so," Packard replied, not looking at her.

"Ooh, like to *do* something with our lives?" Domino joined them with an enthusiastic grin. "'Cause the Army has pixies now. Obviously. Gotta use us for *something*."

"Go." The sergeant renewed his gesture.

"Gladly."

"With pleasure."

"Anything for a change of pace around here, Sergeant."

Z and Domino strode briskly through the open door, shoulders thrust back and chests out. Echo brought up the rear and paused in front of Sergeant Packard, looking him up and down. He took a small step away from her and blinked. Then he surprised them both by pulling rank. "Something you wanna say to me, Private?"

Echo held his gaze, then lifted both hands toward her face. Packard flinched at the movement, but she clearly had no intention of reaching out to touch him. Instead, she brought her fingers to the corners of her mouth and drew them up into a tense, fake smile just like she'd done for him the first day they'd met.

Despite this, Packard managed to form his next words with a lot more authority and confidence than he'd previously had. "I didn't think so. Move."

With a shrug, Echo turned and waltzed into the room.

"Aren't you coming, Sergeant?" Domino asked as Packard went to close the door behind them.

"Never again in my goddamn life," he murmured. "If I'm lucky."

He shut the door with a click, pausing in front of it. It took him a moment to realize he felt like a massive bomb was about to go off.

They just walked right in without a fight. Without asking questions. Without tearing the place apart.

Taking a few slow, deep breaths to calm himself, he pivoted and headed down the hall in search of an elevator that wouldn't stop on every single floor.

Not my job to figure out what they're up to. Not my problem. If nobody can figure out what those assholes are good for, they'll be out of here anyway. And then I'll never have to see another magical again.

Inside the room, the pixies took their time perusing the space around them. Z nodded as she scanned the walls, ceiling, floors, and furniture. "Nice. Looks like we got an upgrade."

"With couches." Domino flopped down onto one of said couches and kicked his booted feet up onto the cushions so he could stretch out all the way. "*Nice* couches. Way better than the dinky mattresses they call beds around here."

"Definitely the nicest room we've been taken to so far."

"I hate it," Echo said flatly.

"Oh, come on." Domino tossed a hand toward her with his other tucked behind his head to cradle it on top of the couch's armrest. "Like you don't like nice things."

"Not *fake* nice things." The goth kicked the cream-colored wall and folded her arms. "This is all fake."

"Would a fake wall make that sound and have a scuff mark after you kicked it like that?" Z asked.

"Obviously, the *wall's* real." Echo folded her arms and looked around the room with calculating eyes. "But we're not here for an upgrade."

"You're right. It's not exactly a five-star resort." Z swiped her finger along the surface of one of the polished bookshelves tastefully decorated with small figurines and plaques she didn't bother to read. Her finger came away without a speck of dust on it, and the corners of her mouth turned up in approval as she shrugged. "But it's a lot better than where they've been making us wait the rest of the time."

"You know what this place could really use?" Crossing one ankle over the other as he sprawled out, Domino raised both hands toward the ceiling in the corner of the room and mimed taking a picture of the same area. "A television box."

"A what?" Z turned toward him and snorted.

"Yeah. For watching movies and stuff. The news, maybe."

"The news is nothing but doom and gloom and how badly humans are screwing each other over." The blue-haired pixie shot her cousin a crooked smile and spread her arms. "Why would you wanna kick back and watch more of *that*?"

Echo thrust a finger in the air. "I'm down."

"Of course you are."

"Fine." Domino dropped his hands, his left landing on his thighs and his right dangling over the side of the couch until his knuckles grazed the carpet. "Just movies, then.

You know, the really good ones. All the superhero stuff, right?"

"Nah, they've got that all wrong." She waved away the idea and headed toward the other side of the room.

"They're movies, Z. How are they gonna get it wrong?"

"I mean, if you're gonna make movies about things that exist, base *some* of it on facts. Like how magic works. And the way some of those weirdos fly... Are you kidding?"

"There's a bunch of movies called *Saw*," Echo murmured. "We should watch those."

Domino slung his arm over the back of the couch and pointed at her. "Yeah, anything *you're* excited about is a definite no right off the bat."

"And *space*," Z continued as she studied the clean, shiny surface of the heavy executive desk on the far side of the room. "Yeah, it exists. Yeah, there are other planets. Obviously. But who has a freakin' spaceship these days?"

"Or *any* days," Domino added with a shrug.

"That's what I'm saying. Forget the TV." She pulled out the executive desk chair covered in well-oiled, cream-colored leather and plopped down into it. A slow smile spread across her lips as she swiveled back and forth and eyed the desk drawers. "They're useless anyway. Remember the last time we screwed around with one of those things?"

"In Boston?" He sat up on the couch and grinned. "Yeah, when Bill tried to take a whole wall of 'em from that electronics store and turned the whole thing into a giant bug-zapper."

Echo popped into her two-inch size and darted toward one of the couch's matching armchairs in a streak of silvery-gray light. When she blew herself back up again, she was already sitting comfortably in the chair with one leg crossed over the other and her arms on the armrests. "That was awesome."

"And that's why we don't need a TV." Z raised her eyebrows at her cousins, giving them a chance to argue with her despite knowing that none of them wanted a TV.

I'm so tired of pretending we have goals right now. But pretending's still better than being blasted back to Oriceran by a grumpy old gnome just waiting for us to break all the rules.

"Besides," she continued as she swiveled back and forth in the office chair again, "Sergeant Packard didn't tell us why we're in *this* room now. But I'm pretty sure it wasn't because someone wants our redecorating skills."

"They should, though." Domino chuckled. "Man, just imagine what we could do with this entire mountain if they let us. Hell, if Calinda and the rest of the gang were still here, we could turn this into a damn amusement park. Pixieland!"

"Pixieland." Z stared expressionlessly at him until he gave in.

"Hey, I've had a lot more time than usual to think about awesome stuff we could do if we were, you know, *doing* anything."

"With swordfights," Echo added.

Her cousin and brother both fixed her with confused frowns.

"To the death."

Z scoffed. "Remind me never to let you make the schedule."

"You never let me make the schedule anyway."

"Maybe that's because the rest of us don't feel like ticking 'blood and gore and death' off our to-do lists every day."

Domino sighed wistfully. "To-do lists. That sounds really nice right now."

"Yeah. *To do*. I'm right there with you." Sitting back in the chair, Z gazed around the room one more time and frowned. "Who do you think this office belongs to?"

"Major Winters?"

"Us?"

"Sergeant Packard's mom?"

They all laughed, but Z couldn't quite get rid of the feeling that something new and different was about to happen. After they finished wasting half the day waiting.

Whatever it is, new and different is way better than absolutely nothing for the rest of eternity. I hope. Or we ended up making this Army deal for no reason.

CHAPTER NINE

For the next two hours, Z and her cousins did what they did best and made the most of the crappy situation they'd been escorted into. They went through every single drawer in the executive desk, which was disappointingly empty save for a few loose sheets of scratch paper and a tin can full of pens. They looked through every book on the bookshelf, but there wasn't anything fun or exciting in them.

Z did end up spending fifteen minutes on a work of historical fiction about some Army general in the early 1900s before tossing it aside. Her cousins thoroughly searched couch and armchair cushions. Ripping the cushions open momentarily sated Echo's desire to wreak havoc and destruction, even if it sent chunks of padding, shredded fabric, and tufts of feathers floating all over the office. There were zero hidden treasures in any of the furniture.

"Man." Sitting on the floor in front of the couch with the last ruined cushion in his lap, Domino pulled his hand free of the stuffing inside it, before tossing it away. "Guess we can check that one off the list too."

Echo lounged comfortably on her back in mid-air. She glanced at her brother, tapped a pen against her lips, then scanned the sheet of paper she'd placed on top of a large book she'd been using as a clipboard. "Which one again?"

"Treasure hunt," he replied dully, brushing a clump of cushion stuffing off the front of his shirt.

"Right." With her tongue protruding in concentration, Echo scratched the pen across the list they'd created of reasons for having been brought to this specific room.

The sound of violent scratching filled the air, and Domino looked up at his sister. "Damn. What did that list ever do to *you*?"

With one more vicious slash with the pen, Echo left the sheet of paper alone. "So there's no confusion."

From her comfy spot in the executive desk chair, Z chuckled. "There's no list anymore, either."

"Well, that was the last one anyway. So I guess you're right." Echo flung the pen, sending it spinning end-over-end across the room. By the time it clattered against the opposite wall and dropped to the carpet, she'd ripped their ideas list into thousands of tiny fragments. She chucked the ripped paper away from her, pointed at the pieces fluttering through the air, and sent a burst of silver light from her fingertip.

Every single shred of paper burst into flames before raining down in a swarm of ash, smoke, and embers.

The flames died when they ran out of material to consume, but the ashy pieces still flickered down onto Domino's hair, his shoulders, and all over his lap and the ripped-open cushion. When the last of his sister's destruction had filtered out of the air, he looked up at her. "Wow."

"You can't leave any evidence behind," she replied, hovering in the air as she folded her hands behind her head. "That's the first mistake every idiot makes. Especially when it comes to hiding dead bodies."

"Great." Domino dusted off his uniform and smacked the couch cushion in an attempt to clean off the ash. "Next time we have a dead body on our hands, I know exactly who to call."

Echo's eyes widened, and she peered over the edge of her invisible hammock at him. "The *next* time? When was the first time?" She looked up at Z. "Why did I not know about your dead body?"

"There wasn't one, Echo." Z dropped her head back against the chair's leather head cushion. "Relax."

It looked like the goth was about to do the exact opposite of what her cousin had suggested, but then she lay back on her magically suspended hammock and sighed. "There's *about* to be one. I can tell you that right now."

"Hey." Domino pointed at her and put on his best impersonation of a disapproving frown. "Just because you feel like having a dead body around doesn't mean that's a good idea."

"Says who?"

"Says the guy who *likes* not having dead bodies around. Watching you massacre literally everything else you get your hands on is more than enough."

"It doesn't count if it's not *breathing*, Dom."

Z tuned out her cousins' pointless argument knowing it would only end up coming back full circle. It had taken them almost two weeks to get to this point, but almost two weeks was clearly their limit. They needed something to do.

So why hasn't Winters given us something yet? He didn't make the OIP just to lock us up for months and drive everyone in this facility batshit crazy, including us.

Her cousins' laughter ripped her out of her thoughts, and she looked up to see crumbling tufts of cushion stuffing flying across the room.

The next handful Domino chucked at his sister flashed with copper light a second before it struck Echo in the cheek as a wet slice of deli meat. He threw his head back and howled with laughter, holding himself around the middle and rocking back and forth on the carpeted floor.

"Serves him right for experimenting on all those poor little Oriceran critters."

Echo peeled the meat off her face, sniffed it, then took a huge bite and chewed. After studying the rest of the slice, she swallowed and shrugged. "I've had better."

"What is it?" Domino shouted through his laughter.

"Bologna." She flung the piece of meat back toward him, and he cracked up again.

The sliced bologna flashed with silver light a second before it landed in Domino's lap. His laughter cut off abruptly as he frowned and picked up the newly transformed item by its forefinger. "A severed hand. Really?"

His sister stared at the hand and the bloody stump at the end of the wrist and smirked. "Makes *me* laugh."

"Wait, so does that mean you just ate a piece of *hand*?" Domino studied the gory object and grimaced in disgust. "Probably tastes like bologna too."

Echo shrugged. "A little."

Z was about to join her cousins in the fun of transforming pillow fluff into something more fun when a pair of quick, shuffling footsteps caught her ear.

That's not out in the hall. It's coming from...behind us?

She jerked upright in the chair and sent a streak of deep-blue light bursting across the room. It struck the bloody hand Domino still held up by the fingertip, and then he wasn't holding severed flesh anymore but just another chunk of cushion stuffing.

"Come on, Z. What gives?"

"Someone's coming."

"Again?"

Echo rolled her eyes. "Maybe if we *let* them see what we're doing when nobody's looking, they'll get off their asses and do something with us."

"Sure. Fill the whole damn room with bloody stumps." After pushing herself out of the chair, Z popped into pixie-size and darted across the office. She pulled up in front of Echo's nose. "See how far that gets you with the gnome when he comes to blast you off the face of the Earth."

Domino snickered. "Literally."

"You too." She pointed at him, and even though her cousin was larger than her in his "make the humans happy" size, the stern warning on her tiny face was enough to get him to toe the line. Z was, after all, the only person in the world who could get them to listen.

"This still sucks," Domino murmured before shrinking down into his natural pixie form and hovering in the air right in front of her. "We need a Plan B."

"Yeah, we can work on that after we work on *this*."

The footsteps she'd heard coming from the other side of the office were even louder now, and the room was a mess.

Z sighed. "Fine. If you guys wanna get caught with your magical pants down—"

"Ooh." Domino giggled. "*That's* embarrassing."

"Then be my guest," she finished. "Or you can—"

The air around Echo popped a split second before the entire room filled with blazing silver light darting back and forth. Z and Domino both blinked against the unexpected glare and didn't have time for any more of a reaction than that.

Because two seconds later, Echo was hovering in the air right in front of them, her black wings quivering as she folded her arms and fixed Z with her unwavering blank expression. "You didn't always talk this much."

Z's mouth popped open. She couldn't decide whether to laugh or draw her cousin into a two-inch fistfight right then and there.

The time for deciding ran out because the footsteps stopped, and the sound of someone jiggling a doorknob filled the room.

Domino pointed at his sister, despite the imminent entrance of yet another Army official. "That was insane."

Echo stared blankly back at him and didn't say a word.

Z scanned the entire room since she'd clearly missed one very important detail. "Where's the *door*?"

"What?" Domino looked toward her as a previously invisible outline cracked open at the back of the office.

It formed a door which, when fully opened, revealed the most suspicious thing in this abnormally nice waiting area were the three Army soldiers standing in a line in the center of the room, each framed by glistening wings in blue, copper, or black. The only oddity was that one of those soldiers had apparently been given permission to walk around in an all-black uniform.

For the newcomer entering the room, nothing else about the view greeting her seemed out of place or remotely off-putting from what she'd been told to expect.

Z and her cousins, on the other hand, were baffled into complete silence when it dawned on them that *this* was the person they'd spent such a long time waiting to see.

CHAPTER TEN

No way. Not another gnome.

That was the first thought racing through Z's mind as the hunched old woman entered. She wore a bright-purple cotton dress and matching sweater, and her steps were uncertain.

Z immediately tossed that thought from her mind because it only took one more second to know the old woman hobbling toward the executive desk while carrying a massive stack of papers tucked under one arm wasn't any kind of magical. She was human.

That shouldn't have surprised her, given where they were and who they usually dealt with, but the resemblance had been so uncanny that Z's vivid imagination had momentarily taken the reins.

Okay, fine. If that old gnome Carmine had a sister, she would be it. Without the psychotic walking stick that makes pixies magicless, but still.

Her cousins were thinking very much the same thing as they stared at the little old lady laying out her stacks of papers and bulging folders. No one said a word since none of them had been able to figure out what was happening.

Z looked at the back of the room to see the hidden door had closed without so much as a click.

Clever. I guess if they can manufacture a bunch of smoke to make us think there's a fire burning this place up from the inside out, they can build a secret door.

The old lady didn't look up from her paperwork as she set it up. Her demeanor suggested both that she'd done this countless times before and that she hadn't yet noticed the three Army pixies standing at attention—or close enough—in front of her.

Domino turned his head to meet Z's gaze and widened his eyes in a silent question. All she could do was shrug and subtly shake her head. *Like I have any idea who this is.*

Echo remained perfectly still, her face a blank mask, then sniffed.

It sounded louder than it should have in the tense silence but wasn't loud enough to catch the old woman's attention. Or if it was, the woman just wasn't interested in acknowledging it.

She finally finished setting up her desk, complete with a small purple calculator, two purple highlighters in different tones, and a purple pen with a fluttering purple feather attached to the top. All of this she'd produced out of thin air because she hadn't brought a bag or purse or briefcase inside with her. Satisfied with the physical arrangement of her things, the woman reached back, grabbed the armrests of the executive chair, and lowered herself onto the leather cushion.

Only after she'd sat down, rolled the chair slightly

closer to the desk, and folded her hands to display her purple-painted fingernails did she finally look up at the baffled human-sized pixies standing in the center of the room.

Z hadn't noticed the woman's glasses until she was looking straight at them. The lenses were massive, perfectly round, and around two inches thick. They magnified her light, gray-blue eyes through the glass. A strand of glittering purple beads fell from one side of them, looped around the back of her neck beneath her short, curly gray hair, and rose back up to attach to the other side. Every time she moved her head, light flashed from the beads in dazzling bursts that were particularly hard for a pixie to ignore.

Echo folded her arms and dipped her chin, staring blankly at the woman.

The newcomer's blue-gray eyes flickered from one pixie face to the next, then she dropped her gaze to the papers on the desk again and gestured toward the armchairs. "Take a seat."

"Um..." Domino let out a nervous chuckle and rubbed his hands together. "I think you walked through the wrong secret door, lady. The library's on the other side of town."

The fact that none of the pixies had any idea where the library was didn't matter one bit.

This has to be some kinda joke. Or the OIP guys just screwed up even bigger than bringing us into the program.

The woman delicately cleared her throat, blinked several times at the paperwork spread out in front of her, and proceeded to speak in a soft, high-pitched voice that wobbled in and out—the perfect real-life version of everyone's little old lady.

"Three Oriceran pixies apprehended six weeks ago exactly, entered willingly into an agreement with the United States Army, specifically the Oriceran Integration Program under Major Henry Winters. Signed and on record, *with* witnesses, as Domino, Echo, and…Z Thornbrook."

After apparently reading all this off her stack of papers, the woman craned her neck to look up at the stunned magicals and blinked at each of them again with comically magnified eyes. "Or are these details incorrect?"

Z glanced at each of her cousins, who returned the same clueless, confused look. "No, you got 'em right. We just…don't know why *you* have them."

With a businesslike sigh, the woman refolded her hands on top of the desk and calmly studied each of them. "My name is Dr. Goldbloom, and I'm here at Major Winters' request to perform your final psychological and character evaluations, after which your commanding officer will receive my recommendations to better place you in the correct MOS for your work with the Army."

The room was so silent that Z thought she could hear Dr. Goldbloom's wrinkled eyelids touching each other when the woman blinked.

Domino snorted, tried desperately to cover it up, and barked another choked-back laugh. "Wait, wait, wait. Hold on."

Z chuckled since she knew where her cousin was going with this and had no idea how the rest of this interaction would play out.

"*You're* here to shrink *our* heads so the *Army* can figure out where to put us? You?"

"Nah." Z choked on another laugh and tried her damnedest to keep a straight face when she added, "I think she's here for the last stage of our training."

"Ha!" Domino smacked his sister's arm with the back of a hand and could barely get the words out between his attempts to stifle more laughter. "No offense, lady, but we're all being played. The Army thinks they can stick the senior citizens in with the pixies to see which one comes out the other side. They have no idea how unfair that is."

"Unfair for me?" Goldbloom asked flatly.

"What? No, for *us*."

"Listen, Doc." Z spread her arms and tried to look humble about what she said next, but it was harder than it looked. "If you're trying to level up your game, you don't wanna start with us. We're… I mean, don't take this the wrong way, but we're kind of elite."

"Went straight into Special Forces," Domino added as he shot Dr. Goldbloom the guns with both hands and grinned. "You know, real top-level stuff."

"You know what, though?" Z looked quickly over her shoulder, then gestured toward the door. "There's a *great* NCO here already who'd be a lot better at pointing you in the right direction. His office is this dinky little closet about five floors down. Sergeant Packard. He's way more your speed."

Domino's braying laughter made it impossible for Z to keep a straight face, and a few more chuckles escaped her as well. Comparing this little old lady with enormous eyes to the pixies' favorite sergeant even got Echo, though she only showed her amusement with a tiny smile as she bobbed her head from side to side and didn't once look away from their new "evaluator."

For all her tiny stature and bug-eyed visage and the color-coordinated comfort items she'd brought with her to make this random desk feel more like home, Dr. Goldbloom was a tough cookie to crack. She didn't react to Z's and her cousin's joking about all the things Sergeant Packard could teach Dr. Goldbloom to do. The hilarity cranked up a notch every time Echo decided to add her thoughts with a quick whisper in her brother's ear.

Instead, Goldbloom glanced patiently at her purple digital wristwatch before tucking it away again beneath the end of her sweater's sleeve. Then she folded her hands on the desk again and stared at the cackling pixies until their hysterics had run their course.

After twenty-two minutes of this, Z checked in on the little old lady sent to evaluate them and noticed just how unaffected she was. She elbowed Domino, chuckled a few more times just to get it out of her system, and decided to meet this head-on. "What's the matter, Doc? You look bored. Are we boring you?"

"I don't have an opinion about these antics of yours one way or the other. If acting this way makes you feel more comfortable about sitting down and committing to an official evaluation, by all means, keep going. Get it all out of your systems. I'll wait."

A laugh burst from Domino's lips before the old woman's words sank in. He kept smiling even through another confused frown as he waited for someone to pop out of the walls at any second and declare this whole thing one giant, ineffective, useless joke because Major Winters couldn't think of a better way to waste all their time. "You want us to keep going?"

"That's up to you," Goldbloom replied without missing a beat.

"But don't you, like, have better things to do?"

"Domino... Can I call you Domino?" When he didn't respond either way, she appeared satisfied just by the fact that she'd gotten all three pixies' attention. "So you're aware, I'm not a regular installation at this military site. Or *any* military site."

"So you're *not* Army," Domino murmured doubtfully.

Z snickered. "Could've fooled me."

Her cousin fought hard to contain another laugh and look serious.

"Major Winters felt that each of your final evaluations required more finesse and a certain level of specialty expertise. Which, apparently, the United States Army just isn't equipped to provide on its own."

"Oh, shit." Z wiggled her eyebrows at her cousins and kept her voice low. Just not low enough for Dr. Goldbloom not to hear. "Private contractor just for us, guys. We're that special."

"All *right*." Bobbing his head to a groovy tune no one else could hear, Domino gave the doctor a thumbs-up. "Now we're talkin', Doc. You're the special shipment for pixie eyes only, huh?"

"Ugh. Come on." Z elbowed him in the side. "It sounds weird when you say it like that."

"Hey, I'm just movin' with the flow, man. Groovin' with the wind. Jiggin' with the vibes."

Echo flicked a finger toward her brother's boots, which instantly crackled with silver light spreading all the way up to his ankles. With a yelp, Domino stepped back, shook out first one foot and then the other, and proceeded to glare at his sister.

"Are we ready to begin?" Dr. Goldbloom asked, briefly spreading her hands in question before folding them again. "Or do you need more time?"

Z narrowed her eyes at the woman. "That feels like a loaded question."

"Every second of our time together is more useful to me than you might expect." The only time the old woman seemed slightly put off by the pixies' behavior was when her gaze flickered toward Domino, who still glared at his sister but now jerked a boot out to the side every few seconds as if he were trying to kick off some kind of creepy-crawly critter that just wouldn't go away.

"Rest assured," Goldbloom continued, her voice wobbly, high-pitched, and fragile-sounding. Her eyebrows drew together in a frown. "I've cleared my schedule for the rest of the day to focus on this time with the three of you. I want you to know that we're going through this at *your* pace. You're calling the shots here."

"Meaning?" Raising an eyebrow, Z tossed a thumb over her shoulder toward the door. "You're totally cool with looking the other way while we bounce?"

"Well, no. I can't say I would either suggest or support such a decision. But I was also under the impression that the three of you didn't have any other pressing engagements to scurry off to. Have I been misinformed?"

"I mean..." Domino shrugged, his usual overconfidence not what it usually was. "We *are* pretty important."

"Excellent. Then let's get to it." Goldbloom gestured toward the armchairs in front of the large desk. Maybe it was supposed to make whoever sat behind it seem that much more intimidating, or maybe that just came from the fact that *this* human wasn't up for playing any of their games, magical or otherwise. "Would anyone like to go first?"

The magical recruits were silent, then Domino sighed and raised a hand. "Yeah, I'll do it."

"Thanks for volunteering, Domino." The old woman nodded at Z and Echo as her first evaluation subject walked dejectedly toward one of the armchairs. "Please leave the room and wait outside. When Domino and I are finished, I'll send him out for one of you."

"Wait, what?" The copper pixies' eyes widened in surprise as he looked over his shoulder at Z. "That's not what I signed up for."

Of course he doesn't wanna be alone with her. If they start splitting us up now, who knows how much they'll try to split us up after we leave this room?

Z nodded at her cousin with as much reassurance as she could muster, knowing Domino had come to the same conclusion. "Take a seat, Dom. Sorry about that."

"That's fine." Dr. Goldbloom returned her attention to one of the stacks of papers on the desk and grabbed a purple pen with the fluttering feather on the end, preparing to get down to business. "Please be sure to close the door on your way out."

"No can do, Doc." Z casually walked around the second armchair placed in front of the desk.

The old woman looked up at her again, her eyes enormous and shimmering through the highly magnified lenses of her glasses, then she tilted her head. "You've never shut a door before? It's fairly simple."

"Sure. But we're not leaving."

Goldbloom hadn't exactly been smiling as she'd gone about setting up her little workstation or confirming the information she already had about the three pixies. Now she was being met with this sort of resistance she clearly hadn't expected, the previous lack of expression on her wrinkled face might as well have been a smile in comparison to the darkening frown she fixed on Z. "These are highly personal and individualized evaluations, Z. For each one of you."

"Aw." Domino's enthusiasm returned as he settled into the first armchair and smiled wide, staring at the stack of papers in front of the doc. "You made that up all special just for me?"

"I did." Goldbloom didn't take her bug-eyed gaze off Z's face. "As well as for Z and for Echo."

"Great." Z plopped down in the armchair beside her cousin's and folded her arms. "Then we can help each other decide if you got things right or not."

After blinking at the blue-haired pixie for a full ten seconds, Dr. Goldbloom sighed and set her purple pen on the desk. "I'm sorry. I see now that when I said 'personal and highly individualized,' I clearly hadn't chosen the right terminology. These evaluations are *private*, Z. The questions are customized for every individual according to preliminary reports on behavior, character, and background information."

"Even better." Z wiggled her eyebrows and smirked.

"Right?" Domino slumped back in his chair and flung both arms up onto the armrests. "Whew. It's about damn time somebody around here started thinking about who *we* are and what *we* want."

"Which is why I insist all evaluations be done *in private*," Goldbloom added.

"Why's that, huh? So there's nobody to call you out on how it went when you lie about it after the fact?"

The woman's eyebrows lifted slightly. Then she returned to the detached expression she'd perfected nearly as well as Echo. "The conversations I'm about to have with each of you have been designed to specifically broach certain subjects each one of you may find…uncomfortable. The fact that the three of you are family raises the probability that the topics, emotions, and ensuing conversations we'll be bringing to light may stir up more conflict than necessary between you. Family dynamics are no joke, especially when—"

"Conflict?" Z snorted.

Domino wagged a finger between him and his cousin. "Between *us*?"

"It's a sensitive—"

"You can save all that for the actual tests, Doc." Smiling, the blue-haired pixie shook her head. "Whatever you think's gonna happen here, you're probably wrong."

"I see." Goldbloom looked at the two pixies wearing self-confident expressions and the third, standing slightly behind them, with no expression whatsoever. "May I ask what makes you so sure of this?"

"What makes *you* so sure?" Domino countered with a cocky little smile and wiggle of his head.

"Fifty-seven years in this field, delivering this exact type of personalized evaluation for thousands of patients," the woman replied flatly.

"Damn. That sounds boring."

"And how many of those patients were *pixies*?" Z added.

The doc didn't miss a beat. "None. You three are the first."

"Well, then, there you go." Z clapped her hands together, then spread her arms and flopped them down on her chair's armrests to perfectly mimic Domino's position in his chair. "I can tell you right now, Doc, we've spent *way* more than fifty-seven years doing everything together, so I think we got you beat there. Plus, we're way older than you."

Goldbloom blinked quickly. "Age isn't necessarily the only qualifier here."

"Hey, none of us know what's gonna happen other than the fact that none of us are leaving this room until you're finished with whatever you came here to do."

The doctor paused a moment longer without giving anything away. "Would you like one more chance to reconsider?"

Domino clicked his tongue and waved the comment aside. "Don't need it."

"Whatever you want us to do," Z added, "we're doing it together. That was the deal with Major Winters, that's the deal with the Army, and you're just gonna have to deal with it."

To further drive the point home, Echo rounded the other side of her brother's armchair and plopped down in mid-air, leaning back and kicking her legs out and folding her arms as if there had been a third chair for her to sit in. She said nothing, and her expression was unchanged.

With a frail-looking shrug, Dr. Goldbloom returned her attention to the paperwork in front of her and picked up her purple-feathered pen again. "I clearly can't change your mind. So let's get started."

Domino thumped a fist on the armrest and grinned. "Bring it."

CHAPTER ELEVEN

Two hours later, Sergeant Balsam stopped in front of the door to the office on G1. He'd received his orders by phone call twenty minutes before to make sure the three obnoxious new soldiers with wings were taken straight back to their sleeping bay to await further instructions.

Whatever Major Winters is dealing with right now, he better figure it out quick. Not like any of us signed up for this assignment, but if we had, it sure as shit wouldn't have been as babysitters for a bunch of fairies.

After checking his watch to make sure he'd arrived in an acceptable length of time, the sergeant reached toward the door with one hand, pausing when he heard something that sounded like crying.

The sound was followed by the noise of a violent nose-blow. Lower, murmured voices followed, though he couldn't make out any of the words. Then a high-pitched wail ensued with two more sharp honks of nose-blowing.

Balsam's already irritated frown deepened even further at the noise. *What the hell's going on in there?*

It wasn't his job to figure that out. Apparently, his only real job for the last two weeks was to take shifts with Sergeant Packard in leading these three new Army freaks back and forth across the facility while Major Winters tried to figure out what the hell to do with them, and just like everyone else who'd been assigned as the major's support staff, Sergeant Balsam couldn't wait to put this particular job behind him.

One step at a time. Get them where they need to go.

Puffing out a sigh and rolling his eyes, he knocked briskly on the door and waited for a response. Instead of a quick "Hello" or "Enter" or some other greeting he'd expected from the private contractor he'd led to this office, he got a loud thump, a sharp smack of flesh on flesh, and another high-pitched wail.

"Not interested!"

"Get lost, pal!"

Balsam frowned even more at the shouted response from the other side of the door. Someone violently blew their nose again, followed by more softly murmuring voices he couldn't understand. So he cleared his throat and tried a slightly different tactic. "It's Sergeant Balsam," he called through the door with another knock. "It's time to—"

"We're busy!"

"Wait your damn turn, Sergeant. We're not done yet!"

He recognized the voices of the only two pixies who ever spoke, and the next voice to rise over the din of what definitely sounded like heartbroken wailing must have belonged to Dr. Goldbloom.

"You're right on time, Sergeant. If you don't mind

waiting just a minute or two longer, we'll be finished shortly."

Balsam stepped away from the door with wide eyes. *That lady's not as calm and happy as she sounds, not after being holed up in a room with those freaks for the last two hours.*

It wasn't just the sergeant's orders making him second-guess the doc's words; he felt a certain responsibility toward the woman. Not needing to protect an elite Special Forces team or any of the other OIP sergeants from three magical morons was one thing, but a civilian contractor old enough to be Balsam's grandma was something altogether different.

So he knocked again. "You sure you're all right in there, Doc?"

"Piss off!" the dude pixie shouted, his voice sounding stuffed up.

"Just a few more minutes, please, Sergeant," Goldbloom called. The high level of confidence in her voice wasn't enough to convince Balsam that everything was okay.

He backed away from the door again and almost gave in to the old lady's request, but then something clanged noisily against the wall. It was followed by a quick succession of more thumps and the sound of something rattling around on the ground.

Honestly, it sounded like someone on the other side of that door was trying to tear the room apart, which only became a more immediate possibility when it ended in a wild, raw, curdling scream. That was the last straw that snapped the sergeant out of his confused indecision and into remembering why he was there.

Those little shits!

His instincts kicked in, and he lunged for the office door before throwing it open. He got all of two steps inside before the warning was already spewing out of his mouth. "I knew it was a bad fucking idea to leave you alone with a—"

"Sergeant Balsam!" Dr. Goldbloom barked as she stood abruptly from the office chair behind the desk. Both of her tiny, wrinkled old hands slammed down on the desk's surface, and she glared at him with enormous, incredulous eyes behind the thick-lensed glasses. "I said a few more minutes."

The sergeant instantly froze since he couldn't fathom the possibility of having been wrong in his assessment of the situation. "But I... It sounded like—"

"Whatever you did or didn't hear is none of your business," Goldbloom added brusquely. "This is a private session, and any sort of unwarranted interruption will not be tolerated!"

"I..." Frowning, Balsam took quick stock of the rest of the room. Dr. Goldbloom was not, in fact, visibly in any immediate danger. She wasn't tied to the chair, hanging upside down by her heels, or buried beneath a pile of rubble, even though that image had gone through the sergeant's head when he'd heard the scream.

Where he'd expected to find the three pixies scattered all over the office amidst shards of glass and broken furniture and the bookshelves in disarray, maybe even laughing as they tortured the poor old lady, the pixies took him by surprise.

Two of them sat in the armchairs in front of the desk while the all-black one lounged in mid-air like she was sitting in an invisible chair. The new recruits maintained such a neat, docile, unimposing line in front of the old lady that Balsam thought his mind was tricking him into seeing things. The pixies didn't look like themselves.

None of them smirked, snickered, laughed in his face, or shot back with a nonsense comment or insult that was obviously meant to goad anyone and everyone into stooping to the magicals' level and engaging. No, now that Z and her cousins had turned in their chairs to look at the sergeant who'd burst in on their private session, Balsam could see that he'd clearly jumped the gun on this one.

Each pixie's eyes were red-rimmed and shimmering as they glared at him. Domino folded his arms, his lower lip trembling. Z clenched her fist around a used tissue and got across the same warning as if she'd crushed a soda can in her hand, though with a lot less noise. And Echo lifted her chin as two lines of silent tears streamed from the corners of her eyes and dripped onto her all-black OCP shirt.

Jesus, this is...

"I hope I made myself clear, Sergeant," Goldbloom added curtly.

"Yes, ma'am." He had to pry his gaze away from the unsettling sight of three pixies openly crying in their armchairs so he could firmly fix it on the old lady instead. "I just wanted to make sure you're—"

"The only thing I need from you right now is a few more minutes and the decency of privacy. Thank you, Sergeant."

The last thing he wanted to do was to turn around and fulfill the doc's request, but what other choice did he have? She wasn't in any immediate danger, and if the pixies had somehow coerced her into lying about it just to stop things from getting any worse, even the best-trained soldiers wouldn't have been able to pull off the same level of confidence and control in her voice.

Plus, three openly sobbing soldiers—magical or not—didn't really suggest *they* were the ones doing the torturing.

The next thing he knew, Sergeant Balsam had stepped back into the hall and pulled the office door shut behind him. As he did so, he realized the agonized wailing he'd heard earlier had come from Domino, who sagged in his armchair with his head thrown back and shoulders shaking.

"That's it, buddy," Z crooned. "Let it all out."

On the other side of him, Echo reached over to give her brother's shoulder two brusque pats in quick succession before pulling her knees up to her chest and wrapping her arms around both legs.

"It feels so *good*," Domino wailed again. The sound was cut off by an abrupt hiccup, then he snuffled and added, "Can I have another tissue?"

"Absolutely." Dr. Goldbloom grabbed a box of tissues off her desk and leaned forward to offer them to him. Her focus was once more centered on her patients and their private session, and she didn't once look back up at Balsam before he'd pulled the door all the way shut with a soft click.

Then he stood there in mute shock as the sound of more muffled crying rose from inside.

What the fuck did I just walk into?

After running a hand through his hair, the sergeant

looked up and down the hallway, confirmed that he was still alone, and leaned back against the opposite wall.

It took more effort than he'd expected to tune out the end of Dr. Goldbloom's session with the OIP's three new magical recruits. The sergeant was so invested in *not* listening to what was happening on the other side of that door that when the door finally did open, it took him by surprise. With a startled jump, he pushed himself away from the wall, straightened stiffly, and cleared his throat.

Holding the door open with one hand, Goldbloom stepped aside and gestured for her latest patients to exit her ad-hoc office inside the facility.

"Okay, Doc, I gotta admit," Z said as she stepped into the hall first. "That was amazing."

"I'm so glad you feel that way."

Domino let out another violent honk as he blew his nose in an already crumpled wad of tissues, then sighed. "Humans. Pixies. Hell, even dwarves, I bet. Doesn't matter what. You're the real deal, Doc. And now you've got us convinced."

"Which is pretty hard to do," Z added, both of them turning sideways as they stepped out of the way so they could both keep the line moving and turn back to eye their unexpected new therapist.

"I think you worked through quite a bit today." Goldbloom nodded over and over as each of the pixies passed her. "So take it easy on yourselves for the next little bit."

"Yeah, no kidding. Hey, Doc?" Domino sniffed again and turned fully to face her. "When do we get to see you again?"

"This was a one-time thing, Domino. I'm sure you understand."

"Yeah, yeah. Sure. But you should really think about opening things up for repeat chats. Even for these soldiers, you know? It'd help them as much as it helped us, and you could charge 'em a shitload to sit down and do *that* with you."

The old woman's face remained perfectly impassive as she stared back at him, though her eyelids fluttered faster than usual. "I already do."

Her surprising composure almost crumbled when she felt a gentle hand settle on her shoulder. Looking quickly up, Goldbloom found Echo standing beside her. The goth stared at the old woman—in gratitude or in warning; it was hard to tell—and let one final tear trickle from the corner of her eye. Then the pixie removed her hand from the doc's shoulder and followed her brother and her cousin into the hall.

Z took a deep breath, feeling refreshed and rejuvenated, and let it all out in a heavy sigh. "So, what now, Doc?"

The woman had already started to close the door but paused when she realized she was still being addressed. "Don't ask me. I came here as a courtesy. Once I've finished my report, Major Winters will find you to share the results of your evaluations."

"Yeah, but..." Domino shrugged and chuckled. "After something like *that*? I mean, what do we *do*?"

Goldbloom looked at the pixies, blinked, and quirked an eyebrow. "Well, I suppose you go do your jobs like everybody else."

"Huh." He scratched his head, and a slow smile of realization spread across his lips. "Yeah. Do our jobs."

"They're all yours now, Sergeant." The doc nodded at Balsam, then stepped back into the office and pulled the door shut behind her.

Only once the door clicked into place did Dr. Goldbloom finally loosen her grip on her composure and self-control. She spun and pressed her back so fervently against the door that it knocked her glasses askew, but she didn't move to straighten them. The woman was too busy taking in deep gulps of air and trying not to hyperventilate as her pulse pounded away inside her like a V8 engine.

Blinking rapidly, she tilted her head back to rest it against the door, being quiet so as not to alert any of the so-called soldiers she could still hear chattering away to each other in the hall. Then she closed her eyes and breathed deeply again since she was pretty sure that trying to keep her eyes open any longer would only bring her to tears that much more quickly.

*Never again. I don't care how much that man's willing to pay me. I will **never** do this again. If I wasn't so old, I'd get out right now and find a new fucking profession.*

CHAPTER TWELVE

Sergeant Balsam hadn't gotten over his shock when Dr. Goldbloom closed the door in his face and handed him the three Army pixies, but he was a firm believer in faking it until he made it. It helped that it was his only option, and his training allowed him to operate on autopilot while he got himself together.

Fortunately, the pixies were in such a good mood that they didn't immediately notice Sergeant Balsam wasn't himself. They even took the lead despite their NCO not telling them where they were supposed to go next.

"I wasn't kidding back there," Domino said as he stuck a thumb over his shoulder toward the now-closed office door. "That should be a requirement of, like...*life*."

"I always thought that kinda thing was a load of crap." Z sighed contentedly and shook her head. "But she proved me wrong. Gotta hand it to her. The doc really knows her stuff."

"We should ask Major Winters to bring her in more. I

mean, if he wants us to be happy little soldiers doing our jobs all the time, he's gotta work to *keep* us happy, right?"

"For sure."

Echo leaned toward her brother to whisper in his ear.

When she was finished, he leaned away with a playful frown. "Don't you think that's jumping the gun?"

She shrugged and stared straight ahead.

"Okay, how 'bout this? We'll *ask* him first. Show him the value of giving us what we want. Give him a chance to make the right choice and loosen up his death grip, yeah? If he still doesn't feel like playing nice after that?" He pointed at his sister and winked. "*Then* you can threaten him."

"Just like the doc said, right?" Z grinned at her cousins. "We have to be *ourselves*. No matter what."

"Best thing ever." Domino shook his head in happy disbelief. "Like, when was the last time anyone ever told us that?"

Echo whispered in his ear again.

"I know, right? Normally, people are encouraging you *not* to give in to the dark side. Including us. Hey, no hard feelings about that, right?"

His sister snorted and stared straight ahead.

While the pixies chatted about Dr. Goldbloom's evaluation, having mistaken it for a therapy session, Sergeant Balsam tuned them out to protect what was left of his sanity.

There's no way that was kosher. She's a little old lady for crying out loud. Whatever she did to make them cry like that...

The idea of being able to do the same thing intrigued him. Balsam let his imagination run wild, except instead of the three pixies sitting in front of a desk and sobbing into tissues, this fantasy involved three magicals strung upside down by their boots over a pit of snakes as they sobbed and wailed, promised to be good little soldiers until the end of time, and begged him to let them go.

He'd zoned out until he found himself in very cramped quarters with all three pixies standing very close, with the chick in black directly behind.

They'd made it into the elevator already?

"What do *you* think, Sergeant?" Domino asked as he folded his arms and shot the young NCO a sidelong glance.

"No comment." Balsam realized how stupid that sounded after he'd said it, but it was the only thing that came to mind, and he had a feeling that if they figured out he hadn't been listening, it would likely ruin the mood for all of them.

"Aw, come on, Sergeant," Z prompted from his right. "Everybody has an opinion."

"And more people should keep their opinions to themselves," he replied, staring at the elevator doors.

"So you don't even care what went on in there?" Domino asked.

"Nope."

"'Cause Dr. Goldbloom's a genius."

"Don't care."

"The best," Z added as she smoothed the front of her OCP shirt. "Wish we could tell you everything, Sergeant. Honest."

"But she made us promise not to say a word to anyone." Domino drew an X over his heart and nodded at the elevator doors. "Doctor-pixie confidentiality and all that."

"Yep." Z pointed at him in agreement. "Very official. Very hush-hush."

"Like, it's totally not okay for us to tell you how fucking *freeing* it is to get in touch with your real emotions."

"Definitely not okay."

Sergeant Balsam swallowed and forced himself to keep staring straight ahead. "Great. So quit talking."

"Sorry, Sergeant. I know it's tough to hear, but we just can't go there."

"Wish we could," Z added, peering past the sergeant to meet her cousin's gaze. "Not possible. You'll just have to deal with the disappointment."

"And you know how much we *hate* to disappoint."

Balsam tried to zone them out again, but now that they were in close proximity, it was much harder to disappear into his private world. He fought against the urge to bounce impatiently on his toes and focused instead on calm, even breathing.

"You know what the doc didn't say anything about?" Z asked, turning to wiggle her eyebrows at Echo.

"I don't know, Z." Domino tilted his head back and forth in consideration. "There wasn't a whole lot we *didn't* cover in there. She really jam-packed those two hours, huh?"

Shit. Balsam pressed his lips tightly together to keep from telling the magicals to just shut up already. *How long have we been in this damn elevator anyway? It shouldn't be taking this long.*

"She never said we couldn't give a *demonstration* here and there," Z continued, mischievous intent creeping into her voice.

Domino gasped in realization. "You're *right*. She didn't mention *that*." He snapped his fingers, then shook an index finger. "See, I *knew* she was a genius."

The elevator lurched to a stop, and Balsam almost sighed in relief. Before the metal doors opened in front of him, he glanced at the little digital screen above them to make sure they were, in fact, getting off on the correct floor.

S1? Why are we stopping here? That's not even close.

"What do you say, Sergeant?" Domino shot the man an enthusiastic wink.

Balsam dropped his gaze to the elevator's control panel to double-check the button. The button for S4 had been pushed and still glowed.

Like all the other buttons on the panel for all the other levels.

"No," Balsam whispered.

"Aw, don't be like that." Smirking, Z nudged him with her elbow as the elevator doors opened. "This'll be fun."

The sergeant had his chance to escape the elevator right then and there. He could have hauled ass down that hallway and found another elevator so he could return to S4 on his own. But he'd also been ordered to make sure the pixies got to their sleeping bay while everyone else involved in the OIP waited to be told what to do next. The chances of the pixies screwing it all up if he ran from them now were all too high.

So were the chances of Sergeant Balsam being in deep shit if they screwed something up because he couldn't do his job.

Pale-faced, he took the worse but more responsible of the two options and stayed where he was.

The elevator doors closed, dooming him to repeat the same process on every floor between here and S4.

"Trust us, Sergeant," Domino said. "You're gonna love this."

Sergeant Packard heard the unearthly wailing and pounding coming from down the hall seconds before the air filled with a high-pitched ding and the elevator doors opened. He stopped midstride and turned just as the doors slid apart enough to reveal one terrified-looking Sergeant Balsam surrounded by the three pixies.

Z slammed a fist repeatedly against the elevator wall and let out sharp, screaming grunts. Domino threw his head back and howled at the elevator ceiling, shaking his upturned hands in obvious grief. Echo stood perfectly still at the back of the elevator, one arm hanging at her side while the other let off an occasional burst of silver light that crashed into the top of the elevator and made all the lights flicker.

What the actual fuck?

Packard stared at the off-putting scene and couldn't figure out what to do as Balsam hurriedly squeezed himself through the elevator doors. The man looked like he was being charged by an enemy instead of stepping off an elevator, and his panic was slightly contagious.

"Hey," Packard called toward him, then had to clear his throat. "What happened?"

Balsam looked surprised to be addressed by another human being, but seeing Packard standing in the hall made him pull up out of his desperate sprint until he was speed-walking down the hall. "Where the hell have you been?"

"I..." Packard frowned and peered past the other NCO to see all three pixies walking out of the elevator. "Went out for lunch."

"Well, you fucking took long enough. Did you get Major Winters' last message?"

"What message?"

"*Hey*, Sergeant Packard," Domino called. Even with tears still streaming down both cheeks, the copper pixie grinned at their favorite NCO and wiggled his fingers in a playful hello. "Fancy seeing *you* here."

I work here. Packard was about to say it out loud, but Sergeant Balsam reached him and clapped a hand down on his shoulder. "He wants that report sent over to his desk ASAP."

"Who?"

"Major Winters."

Packard let Balsam lead him down the hall but couldn't help looking over his shoulder at the pixie trio casually following them. "What report?"

"You know, the fucking report," Balsam hissed. He dug his fingers into Packard's shoulder and picked up the pace. "Can't remember the name of it, but I'll know it when I see it."

"Sergeant Balsam, I don't have any reports ready for—"

"Bullshit. You're always prepared for everything. So we're going to your office. Alone. To get Major Winters what he needs."

"Sergeant Balsam," Z called, cupping both hands around her mouth despite the fact that everything echoed very well inside these walls, "you're taking off before the best part!"

"Yeah, you don't wanna miss this bit," Domino added as he shook a finger in Echo's direction. "Honest."

"Hey, maybe Sergeant Packard wants to stick around for the rest of it."

"The rest of what?" Packard made the mistake of trying to turn back toward them, but Balsam's fingers dug painfully into his shoulder, and he gave Packard a shake.

"Don't fucking look *back* at them. Are you crazy?"

"But they're obviously up to—"

"At this point, I really don't give a shit. Either we get to your office so I can breathe, or I murder everyone in this fucking building. Got it?"

"Wow. You guys are really booking it," Z called. "Miss an important meeting or something?"

"Hey, if you need any help, Sergeants, just say the word and—"

"Get back to the bay!" Balsam shrieked before he whisked Packard around the next corner.

"You got it, Sergeant!"

"We're on it!"

"You can count on us!"

Echo whispered in her brother's ear.

"Oh, yeah. She says don't forget to let it all out every once in a while!"

Though both NCOs had disappeared from sight, the pixies knew Balsam and Packard could still hear them.

Z and her cousins couldn't stop laughing as they

followed their usual route to the sleeping bay. They could have done it in their sleep, and though Sergeants Balsam and Packard had raced off to put as much distance as possible between themselves and the magicals, they weren't far enough away to mask the echoing crack of a door slamming shut in another branching hallway just ahead.

"Oh, man." Z wiped tears of laughter from the corners of her eyes and sighed. "I had no idea you could cry on demand like that, Dom."

"Hey, until Dr. Goldbloom, nobody's ever given me a reason to try."

"We shouldn't have let him get off the elevator," Echo murmured, narrowing her eyes at where Balsam and Packard had disappeared. "I would've gotten him to cry."

"Meh. It just takes more finesse." Her brother nudged her in the arm. "You'll get there."

They turned the corner, and Z thoughtfully scanned the walls and ceiling of the corridors. "Seriously, though. Where *is* Winters? Everyone's been throwing his name around all day, but he hasn't shown up yet."

"Why?" Domino raised an eyebrow but failed to hide a smile. "You got a hot date or something?"

"I just hope he didn't, you know…end up in some kinda *terrible* trouble."

Echo pounded a fist into her opposite palm and growled, "'Cause that's *my* job."

Before the pixies could say anything, a loud thump

came from the direction of Sergeant Packard's makeshift office.

"What the actual fuck!" the sergeant screamed, followed by more banging and the sound of several heavy items falling off the shelves around him. "No. No, no, no. I didn't do this. How the hell did… Oh, you've got to be kidding me."

Z and her cousins exchanged knowing looks as they strode down the hall and waited for the grand finale.

Packard's office was silent, then the explosion they'd been anticipating came.

"Those flying motherfuckers!"

One right after the other, the pixies shrank before zigzagging and spiraling down the hall in a flurry of high-pitched giggles and trails of multi-colored light.

CHAPTER THIRTEEN

The metal double doors to the pixies' sleeping bay burst open, and three streaks of colored light darted across the room—deep blue, copper, and muted silver-gray. Domino and Echo were still laughing as they looped and fluttered all over the room, but Z had only one thing in mind.

Hopefully, we freaked everyone out enough today to leave us the hell alone for longer than ten minutes.

She raced toward her double bunk, which made up one-third of the bunk circle she and her cousins had created here during their OIP Bootcamp. It made things feel more like home, which was wherever they laid their heads. For now, that was here.

Z wasn't even remotely interested in sleeping.

Before the double doors had finished swinging shut, she'd flown to the metal drawer beneath her bunk. Though she and her cousins had officially graduated, Major Winters had failed to provide them with any upgrades, including to the monotony of a life of doing nothing and being *tested* on it.

Not gonna let that keep happening. Packard's pissed, Balsam's terrified, and Winters is apparently missing. Might not have this kind of chance again soon.

Slamming open the drawer under her bottom bunk, Z dove in head-first to rustle through the few personal belongings she had. By the time she finally zipped back up out, treasure in hand, Domino and Echo had fluttered to the triangle of empty floor in the center of their bunk circle, still cackling away.

"They're doing it to themselves!" Domino managed to squeak out.

Stretching her glistening black wings to their fullest span, Echo flipped upside down and walked across the linoleum floor on her hands, twirling and dipping and making shapes with her body just for the fun of it. "Buncha clowns. That's who we work for."

"Yeah, but these ones have no idea how hilarious they are. And no, Echo. You *can't* tell them."

Neither of the siblings was aware of their younger cousin zipping toward them, so when the thick, heavy envelope dropped down onto the floor with a loud slap, Domino and Echo both paused what they were doing to take a look.

"Ooh." The copper pixie tilted his head. "What's that?"

Z landed squarely on both feet, then sent a bolt of deep-blue light into the enormous envelope. The whole thing bounced in the air, flipped over, and landed with the bright-red Oriceran symbol facing up.

"Oh." Domino sighed and propped one hand under his chin. "That again."

"Damn right." Z crossed her legs beneath her and

pointed at the envelope again. "It's time to figure out what's inside this thing."

Another bolt of blue light darted toward the stolen envelope.

"Whoa, whoa, whoa." Domino sent a copper streak of magic through the air. It struck the bulging envelope a split second before his cousin's and sent the thing skittering away. Z's magic cracked against the floor and fizzled out.

Z glared at him, raising her eyebrows.

Domino shrugged. "Let's maybe talk about this first, huh?"

"There's nothing to talk about, Dom."

"Well, we'll just have to agree to disagree about you being right." He took a moment to go over what he'd just said, then nodded. "Meaning you're wrong."

"No, I'm not." Z sent another dart of blue light toward the envelope, thinking she'd be faster this time, but he beat her to it again.

The envelope spun and skittered toward Echo. Still walking upside down across the floor, she lifted one hand just in time to avoid having it knocked out from under her. She craned her neck to look at her brother and cousin, who ignored her silent balancing act and the retreating envelope to face off with each other.

"Come *on*," Z hissed. "What gives?"

"Oh, I don't know. Just a few shits." Domino folded his arms. "Which I honestly expected *you* to give, but I guess I was wrong about that, too."

"What?"

He pointed at the envelope that had gone under one of the bunks. "You really think it's a good idea to open that thing right here in the bay? It's got Oriceran magic written all over it. Literally."

"Yeah, without the literal part. It's just a symbol, Dom. One bright-red stamp on the front."

"We don't know that for sure, though." Folding his arms, Domino fixed her with the same 'I dare you' stare normally used by Z. "And maybe this doesn't qualify for *you*, but *I'm* pretty sure opening a bunch of magic we don't know anything about while we're *inside a mountain* is something that would probably bring the old gnome back to check on us."

Z scoffed. "I promise there's no magic in that symbol."

"Woah." Her cousin lifted both hands and stared at her, open-mouthed. "Now *you're* making promises you can't keep?"

"Fine." Rolling her eyes, she gestured toward the envelope and decided to play his game. "Say there's the tiniest sliver of magic on that thing that I somehow failed to notice when I was carrying it *in my pocket*. What's it gonna do, huh?"

"Hypothetically? No clue." Domino wiggled his head at her in sarcastic defiance. "For all we know, it could blow the top off this entire mountain the second we lift *one* tiny corner."

At that fun idea, Echo's eyes widened. She spun gracefully on one hand to face the envelope and grinned. "I'm on it."

She darted toward the hypothetical threat in a streak of dull silver light before her brother and cousin even knew what was happening.

"It's not gonna blow up the entire mountain," Z continued. "Or even part of it. It was in a safe deposit box in a bank, for crying out loud. A *human* bank."

"Ha. Nice try, Z. But we all know there's no such thing as a bank for magicals and their stuff."

"And you really think somebody would be dumb enough to put a dangerous magical stamp inside a human bank?"

"Hell yeah, I do. Humans do all kinds of weird crap I couldn't explain even if I wanted to."

"All right, I'm not arguing with you on that one. But come on, Dom. I've wanted to do this since we got here. And since when have you been scared of mystery and excitement, huh?"

Domino pursed his lips and turned away. "Since mystery and excitement might turn out to be the old gnome's personal hotline. I'm pretty sure he had no idea that thing was even on you."

"Yeah. That's the point."

While they argued, Echo picked up the envelope and zipped out from under the bed, holding it over her head with both hands. She darted to the ceiling, smirked at her oblivious brother and cousin, and ripped open one corner.

She grinned at the potentially explosive package, but when nothing happened, she scoffed and rolled her eyes.

"This isn't even remotely the most insane thing we've done since signing this Army deal," Z insisted. "But now that envelope worries you?"

"Well, maybe I got comfortable!" Domino blurted. "Did you ever think of *that*? Huh? Maybe I don't *want* something mysterious and exciting falling down on all our heads when we least expect it."

With perfect timing, the overly-full envelope dropped from the ceiling to land between them.

Domino stared at it, then let out an uncertain chuckle. "No shit."

Z looked up to see Echo floating back to the floor, her arms folded and a look of intense boredom once more marring her features. "If you were trying to make some kinda point, Echo, I'm pretty sure I missed it."

"Not my fault," the goth murmured. "Maybe next time, don't get my hopes up."

"About what?" Domino shouted, then it dawned on him, and he gaped at her before looking at the envelope. "Oh, the exploding-magic part. For the love of *not dying...* you *opened* it?"

"You're the one who played it up like it would be exciting." With a snort, Echo kicked the edge of the envelope and sent it spinning toward Z.

This time, the blue-haired pixie didn't have to zap it or risk Domino intervening to make sure she didn't. She stopped the envelope by stomping on it, and there was no denying that one end of the fully stuffed package had been ripped away.

"Okay. So there's no point arguing about the magic part now." Z indicated the envelope and shot Domino an exasperated look. "There isn't any."

"Should've started with *that*," Echo grumbled, "Instead of all the conjecture. Which was really misleading, by the way."

Domino turned to his sister. "Well, *now...*"

"Yeah. Major letdown."

Ignoring the spiteful glare her cousins exchanged, Z

pointed at the envelope and zapped it one more time. The envelope skittered off to the right, and the package's contents bounced off to the left as the pixie's magic crackled over it from top to bottom. The thickly folded stack of papers that slid out unrolled itself, revealing the mystery package's contents.

Rubbing her hands together, Z scanned the document, eyes widening by the second.

"Okay, Well, if it's not magic," Domino stated, stomping toward her, "It's gotta be something good. You only make that face when it's something good."

"What are you talking about?" Echo spread her arms but stayed where she was. "Nothing exploded."

"Nope." Z folded her arms, pursing her lips as she studied the top sheet of paper. When Domino stopped beside her, they looked it over together with identical expressions of curiosity, tilting their heads first to the left and then to the right at the same time. If anyone else had seen it, the mannerism would have magnified the family resemblance.

The only person present, however, was Echo, and she didn't find it very amusing. Rolling her eyes, the goth sighed and threw herself back like she'd finally consented to a round of trust falls. Of course, the only person she had to trust was herself, and she didn't let herself down, her glittering black wings and her magic stopping her from slamming into the floor. She hovered there and pretended not to care about the new mystery Z had found.

Their curiosity was short-lived once they'd figured out what it was they were looking at.

"Well." Domino scratched the side of his head and raised his eyebrows. "That was anticlimactic."

"Oh, come on. You were freaking out two seconds ago."

"Yeah, but now there's no explosions, no magic, and no fun. This is—"

"Boring human stuff. Yeah, I get it."

Because it was. After all the buildup and the time Z had spent imagining what would happen when she finally got enough time to look at what made this package so important to the human she'd stolen it from—and why a human had stamped an Oriceran symbol on it in the first place—the reality was incredibly underwhelming.

More than that, it was downright disappointing.

"This can't be everything," she muttered before sending a burst of blue light at the folded papers. The top page fluttered and flipped over, so she skimmed the next page. The second, third, and fourth pages were all more of the same nonsensical business jargon. A third of the details were redacted, as well as nearly all the numbers on something that looked like a bank statement.

"Boring human stuff," Domino echoed in surprise, then nudged his cousin with an elbow. "You got all bent outta shape about a bunch of *boring human stuff!*"

"Shut up."

"Oh, shit." He broke into a devious grin, then turned to his sister. "You seeing this? Our baby cousin, little blue-haired pixie bomb over here, got every human we know right now frazzled and distracted and out of her way so she could go over the freaking *quarterly reports*! And I haven't even seen a single quarter in here yet."

Echo stared at her brother, then turned her dark gaze

on Z. One corner of her mouth twitched in distaste, followed by her nose wrinkling. The rest of her face remained impassive. "Pathetic, Z."

"Don't." Blue light streamed from Z's finger as she kept flipping through the pages, searching fervently for something that would make all the mental energy she'd put into getting to it worthwhile.

"Hope the Army hasn't made you soft already."

Domino laughed and pointed at his sister. "Exactly! 'Cause if we're there right now, what the hell happens next, huh? Your big amazing goal got debunked on the first try like a popped balloon."

"Like a ruptured spleen," Echo added.

"Or that." Domino frowned at her, then shook his head and continued. "Face it, Z. You got curious, and then you got bored. Sometimes stupid human crap is just stupid human—"

"Nobody asked for your opinion," Z snarled, barely noticing when her cousin lifted both hands and turned away to show he wasn't that invested in keeping up the argument he thought he'd won. She was too focused on her anger and disbelief and the niggling feeling in the back of her mind that there was something else here.

There has to be. The only humans who know enough about magicals to know what a freaking Oriceran symbol is are the ones stuck in this mountain with us. And the FBI, I guess. Whatever they're supposed to be good for. There's no way this is just a minor thing. Humans aren't supposed to have this kinda stuff on them. Not even in their safety deposit boxes...

When her irritation finally grew too strong for her to hold back, she whisked a hand toward the half-overturned stack of stapled papers as if she were slapping someone in the face. A bark of frustration and anger escaped her lips. The packet crackled with blue pixie light, and the pages fluttered rapidly away from each other one by one like they were being battered about by a strong wind. A pixie's anger was strong, but Z just wanted to get rid of the thing.

Fine. I can admit when I was wrong. Doesn't mean I don't get to be pissed as hell about it.

She was on the verge of sending another crackling blast right into the center of the fluttering packet and lighting the whole thing on fire. Echo would've approved, which would then make Domino outnumbered if he decided to argue with her about *this* decision too.

Before she could act on that impulse, though, a much smaller projectile launched out of the packet from between two pages and hurtled straight toward her face.

She yelped in surprise and blocked the flying object with a swift toss of her forearm. That kept it from striking her full in the face, but the impact of being hit sent her staggering back until she leapt into the air and hovered there to get a better view.

Domino barked another laugh and stared at his cousin, ignoring the projectile. "Oh, *shit*."

Echo folded her arms and allowed herself a tiny smirk. "Now *that's* what I'm talking about."

Z glanced at the forearm she'd used to deflect whatever had come from between the pages. It ached, but if constantly wearing Army-issue OCPs was enough to protect her from unexpected envelope attacks, it had served its purpose. "What the hell was that?"

"It went that way." Echo stuck a thumb over her

shoulder but didn't turn around to find the item or offer to help retrieve it.

With an aggravated sigh, Z fluttered higher to get more perspective. She stopped and pointed when she saw it. "That? *That's* what flew out of the papers and tried to take my arm off?"

Domino found what she was pointing at and broke into a crooked smile. "You know, something tells me none of this was put together with pixies in mind."

"Yeah, nothing ever is."

CHAPTER FOURTEEN

It was a business card.

That seemed like the dumbest thing in the world when Z fluttered down beside it and stared at the blank, off-white surface staring back.

Now that this new piece had revealed itself, she couldn't just burn it right along with the whole packet, so she blasted the card with another bolt of deep-blue light and flipped it over in the hopes the other side wouldn't be just as blank.

For the first time since opening the envelope, Z wasn't disappointed.

"No way." Domino half-walked, half-fluttered over and landed on the other side of the business card to stare at it upside down. "That's a calling card. Like, literally."

He didn't have to point at the slightly raised numbers embossed with glossy black ink on this side of the card. Those numbers were impossible to ignore when they took up a third of the empty space there. The other two-thirds belonged to a single word embossed in the same font and the same glossy black ink—Arbitum—and above that, a neatly stamped symbol in a bright blood-red hue.

Z cocked her head, studied the symbol above the phone number, then started to turn back to the rest of the package.

"It's the same," Echo said with a curt nod. "Promise."

"Obviously." Folding her arms, Z fought down the overwhelming urge to go check for herself in case her cousin felt like screwing with her.

That's just an excuse to start acting like a jerk, Z. Don't. They're both as serious as you are right now because you just proved there was something useful here after all.

Now she just had to figure out what that was.

"So." Domino looked back and forth between his sister and cousin, then shrugged. "What's Arbitum?"

"Oh, yeah. That's right." Z thrust a finger in the air as a direct impersonation of him when he felt like being a smartass, which was more often than not. "I forgot I already know everything about this and was just playing around with you for fun."

He studied her, then narrowed his eyes and pointed at her. "I knew it."

"That's not usually how those things are supposed to work, right?" Echo asked.

Z looked up at her cousin's approach. "What, business cards?"

"*Calling* cards," Domino corrected.

"No, Echo. I'm pretty sure they're not supposed to launch flying attacks out of secret human business packets."

The goth rolled her eyes in a slow, exaggerated arc, and

another tiny smile flickered at the corners of her mouth. "I mean, don't get me wrong. I'm a fan of *that* part."

"Uh-huh."

"I mean the stuff that's on there." Echo pointed at the card and wiggled her finger. "Don't humans put all their useless personal information on these things?"

"Huh. Yeah." Domino frowned as he considered the implications. "They do seem *really* into telling everybody their whole life's story right up front without having to look people in the eye."

Z and Echo stared at him in bafflement, then Z cleared her throat. "I think she's talking about the contact info."

He wrinkled his nose and spread his arms. "Yeah. So am I."

"Okay, Dom. Well, *this* card doesn't have a name, title, address, or email. Nothing. No identifying information other than that phone number. And whatever Arbitum is."

"And the giant red symbol you've been going on and on about. Obviously."

"Obviously." Z watched her cousin for any sign that he was aware of how ridiculous he sounded, but Domino was in one of his serious and contemplative moods. She couldn't help smirking as she folded her arms and turned her attention back to the business card that didn't say anything about a business or even what it was for. "Too bad we haven't gotten our standard-issue Army cell phones yet."

He whipped his head up to frown at her. "I don't even know how to use a cell phone."

"Can't be all that different from a regular phone," Echo observed. "The numbers are the same."

"Yeah, but I don't know how to use a regular phone, either."

"We can work on that." Z clapped a reassuring hand down on her cousin's shoulder. "*After* we figure out what a human was doing with this weird contract and a card from Arbitum in his safety deposit box."

"Because…humans do weird shit and have no idea what it's about until it's too late?"

"Not gonna argue with you there, Dom. But I was referring more to the whole 'Oriceran symbol on all this paperwork' thing."

"Oh." The copper pixie squinted at the card on the floor, then stuck a pinky in his ear and wiggled it around to get rid of an itch. "Maybe the guy isn't human?"

"What are you talking about?" She scoffed, looked up at Echo to see if her other cousin thought the sentiment was as ridiculous as she did, then remembered Echo was the last person to look to for visual cues. "We already went over this. Of course the dude's a human. We robbed a human bank."

"Yeah, and we're pixies in the Army. So?" Domino fixed her with an exaggerated grimace and shrugged.

"Right. I guess we already went over all that too, huh?"

"Just a little."

After another moment of staring at the red Oriceran symbol on the business card above the word and then at the phone number beneath it, Z sighed and finally had to admit that taking a win here was the only option she had. "Fine."

With a soft pop, she ballooned into normal human size, picked the card up off the floor, and took it with her. She also retrieved the nonsensical "secret contract" and the envelope that had started it all.

"What are you doing?" Domino asked.

"I'm putting this stuff away." It took some maneuvering to get the enormous stack of papers and the business card back in the envelope, but once she finished, she tossed the whole thing back into the storage drawer and kicked it shut. The metallic clang echoed around the bay as Z flopped onto her bunk on her back. She kicked her feet up, crossed one ankle over the other, and stared at the underside of the bunk above.

"Wait, wait. Hold on." Another soft pop sounded as Domino went from two inches to five-foot-nine. He spread his arms as he walked across the center circle toward her. "You're giving up already? Just like that?"

A sharp laugh escaped her as she looked at her cousin. "First it's, 'Don't open the envelope!' Then it's, 'Let it go, Z. It's just a dead end.' And now you're going with, 'You can't give up just like that?'"

He stopped a few feet from her bunk and clicked his tongue. "Yeah. That's what I'm going with."

"You really need to work on your flip-flopping, Dom."

"Really? I think I'm doing a pretty great job of it."

That made her laugh again. Then they were distracted by the silver-gray light streaking toward another of the bunks. Echo darted over the bottom bunk, then popped into human size and dropped onto her back onto the mattress.

"And I guess *you* need help reading between the lines," Domino continued, ignoring his sister's antics. "I'll spell it out for you, Z. You can't just let this go because that's not what you *do*."

"Even though you were arguing against it from the beginning."

Domino grinned. "Because that's what *I* do."

They laughed at that, then Z kicked off her boots, let them topple one after the other onto the floor, and folded her hands behind her head. "No, Dom. I'm not just gonna let this go. 'Cause there's something weird about this whole thing, and if it doesn't have some perfectly reasonable explanation, I need to figure out what's going on."

"Curiosity killed the cat, you know," Echo murmured from her bunk.

Z pointed at her. "Yeah, but not the pixie. So we still don't have anything to worry about."

"Wait." Domino stepped back so he could look between them. "Who said anything about killing?"

Echo stared blankly at the underside of the bunk above her and raised her hand. "Me, probably."

"No, I mean cats. *Who's* killing cats?"

"Nobody, Dom." Z tried not to laugh as she watched her cousin trying to puzzle out exactly what that meant. "It's another human saying."

"Well, *now* you tell me." He ran a hand through his messy auburn hair, then clicked his tongue in disappointment. "I thought it was, 'Curiosity *kicked* the cat.' Which really isn't any better, but at least the cat's still *alive*. Shit."

Distressed by this new revelation, Domino stalked back and forth, mumbling to himself and occasionally kicking at thin air before frowning and trying to reason it out all over again.

Echo rolled onto her side to face Z's bunk and propped her head in one hand. "So I just ripped open the same can of worms, huh?"

"Oh, for crying out loud!" Domino shrieked as he whirled toward her. "Now we're ripping up *worms*?"

The other pixies ignored what they both knew was just another rhetorical question.

"Yeah, I guess so," Z replied. "Same can, just better lighting. We're gonna keep looking because I really don't like the idea of some other organization bringing on a bunch of random humans with bad taste in watches."

She and Echo both snickered, but Z was only half-joking.

"It's not FBI stuff. It's obviously not Army stuff. And beyond that, I can't think of a good reason to throw humans and Oriceran magic together in the same boat. So we're gonna figure out who's doing it and why."

"How's that exactly?"

"I mean, it's obviously not that hard to get a hold of *somebody's* phone in this place."

The inference to Sergeant Packard's office and the makeover they'd given it ripped Domino out of his frustrated mumbling, and he stopped pacing.

"We wait for a good time to make a phone call and hope it goes right to Arbitum." Z picked at the balls of lint collected on the outside of her blanket. "Or we could ask around. See if anyone else knows what that symbol stands for and why it might've ended up with a human."

"Ask around?" Echo asked. "Oh, you mean like Major Winters?"

The bay fell silent, then all three pixies laughed at the

thought of any of them asking the major for help with anything, let alone a private affair that barely had anything to do with magic. At least, not as far as they could tell.

"I would *love* to see that," Domino managed after the laughter died down. "It'd be worth it just to see the look on his face when he thinks we're *joking*."

"Winters doesn't have anything to do with it." Z was certain of that since the man had been so reluctant to make this deal with three rogue pixies. There was no conceivable way he would want anything to do with Oriceran symbols or hiding magical things in a regular bank. He didn't even want anything to do with the three magicals currently under his command.

"Besides," she continued, "the Army needs *us* and *our* help. Not the other way around."

"Well, duh." Domino spread his arms and turned to survey the bay. "I mean, just look at the state of things in here. If they'd just let us take over with the decorating…"

Echo took a sharp breath, then pushed into a sitting position and let her black boots dangle over the edge. Her eyes widened in realization, and a slow smile spread across her lips. "You wanna start sneaking out again."

"Wow." Domino plopped down on his bunk, leaned forward, and propped himself up with his forearms on his thighs as he shot his sister a frown. "You got *that* from 'the Army needs our help?'"

Echo ignored him and kept staring at Z. "But, like, *out*-out this time."

Z shrugged and pretended not to be excited about the prospect. "I mean, it's not like we're gonna find any other magicals walking around inside a mountain. Not *this* mountain, anyway."

"Wait, what do we need other magicals for?"

"Expanded horizons, Dom." Z laughed at her cousin's clueless expression and fought the urge to make him figure it out for himself. "We're not the only magicals on Earth. And if there's some weird Oriceran group out there recruiting humans for…whatever, I bet we're not the only ones who know about it. At the very least, someone's gotta know what that symbol means."

"Who, like the gnome?"

Z and Echo groaned and rolled their eyes at the thought of asking Carmine Ratchetter for help with anything, even if they had known where to find him.

"Don't say stuff like that," Echo grumbled.

"Then who are you guys talking about?"

"Literally any other magicals, Dom. They're out there, and when we finally get out of this stupid mountain, we'll have more chances to go find them and get a few answers for a change. Maybe pull off one hell of a job in the process, right?"

"Ooh, yeah. I like that." Domino wagged a finger at Z and studied the bay's ceiling as he imagined the results. "Military pixies ripping off hella greedy Oricerans who think humans are smart enough to run with the big kids."

That set them all laughing again, and none of them thought twice about the fact they were also Oriceran magicals working with humans—smart enough or not.

CHAPTER FIFTEEN

Though the pixies had something new and exciting to focus on—like how to investigate this so-called Arbitum group putting Oriceran-magic symbols and humans together like a bag of trail mix—it still wasn't enough to distract Z and her cousins from their day-to-day lives. It quickly became clear that in their daily lives as part of the OIP, something wasn't quite right.

For almost two weeks now, they'd been existing in limbo, and that was all well and good for everyone involved until the facility's temporary mess hall stopped serving food.

"Well, shit." Domino tossed his hands in the air and faced Z and Echo. "You know, I could handle it when they took away our friends. No Alpha Team? No problem. But now it's the chow too? That's not how to win pixies over, lemme tell ya."

It wasn't just the lack of food that was slightly disturbing. The three banquet tables normally set up on the far side of the room were gone, along with all the tables and chairs where the three pixies had gotten used to sitting.

"I knew it," Echo murmured flatly. "They're trying to kill us."

"Right. Because that would definitely be in their best interest." Z rolled her eyes. "Maybe the guys cooking just…figured we'd already left by now."

"We were definitely supposed to, right?" Domino shook his head as he followed his sister and cousin out of the empty hall. "I mean, that's what everybody's been saying lately. Not in so many words, of course, but there was definitely an implication."

"Maybe they all just…got held up by traffic or something."

"Is there even traffic this early in the morning?"

"How should *I* know? We don't drive."

Z and her cousins dejectedly made their way through the facility's hallways, their stomachs grumbling and their imaginations running wild with all the reasons they weren't being fed this morning the way their contract with the US Army had assured them they would be.

"Maybe it's another test," Z mused. "Like they wanna see what we'll do without the basic necessities."

"Or maybe they're trying to kill us," Echo repeated with a shrug.

Her brother and cousin fixed her with disapproving frowns, then Domino asked, "Hey. Who's the one person around here who knows everything about what's happening with everything else and when?"

They stopped to share a mischievous smile before shouting, "Sergeant Packard!"

It didn't take them long to get to the sergeant's cramped little office. Z reached the closed door first and delivered three brisk knocks.

"Just a second," Packard called from the other side. "I'm in the middle of—"

Z jerked on the handle and threw open the door before he could finish. "Sergeant Packard!" she exclaimed as if he was the one who'd just barged in on *her* personal space. "Just the guy we were hoping to see."

"No." He wagged a finger at her and shook his head as she walked into his office. "Get the hell out."

"We just wanted to come visit our favorite sergeant," Domino added as he and Echo followed.

"Don't call me that," Packard grumbled. "And I'm not *taking visitors*. I don't even wanna *look* at you right now."

Domino giggled and stuck his hands on his hips. "I love it when you play hard to get."

"We ran into a problem this morning, Sergeant," Z began, willing to bring up the issue of no food with a pleasant disposition and a healthy dose of humor. "Went down to the mess hall at our regular time."

"You know, *chow time*," Domino added.

"And it looks like somebody forgot to do their job. So we figured we'd come ask you what that's all about, you know?"

"The mess hall." Packard stared at her, glanced at Domino and Echo, then blinked furiously before his scowl deepened. "That's what you wanna talk to me about? The fucking mess hall? I don't know, guys. Maybe it's because you three morons were supposed to be out of here already and stuffing your stupid faces somewhere else. How's that sound?"

"I mean…" Z patted her stomach. "Sounds amazing. We're hungry. Any chance you could—"

"No."

"Well, what about—"

"No."

Z rolled her eyes, sighed, then met Echo's gaze and stuck a thumb out toward the sergeant like he couldn't see her silently referencing his bad move.

"Sergeant." Domino stepped toward the desk, and Packard straightened, then leaned as far back as he could as the copper pixie kept walking toward him. When Domino stopped, he walked his fingers across the surface of the small desk and casually propped a leg and half his backside on the edge of the furniture before smiling down at the NCO. "What do you mean we were supposed to be out of here already?"

"Don't do that." Packard glanced at the pixie's uniformed leg on his stuff and pushed himself even farther back in his chair. "Don't sit on my stuff."

"I won't if you tell us what we wanna know."

"Please. Like you don't already know what that means." The sergeant scoffed, but when none of the pixies said or did anything else, he realized they weren't trying to mess with him. "Seriously? Jesus. Okay, look. We were *all* supposed to be on our way out to new posts this morning. The whole OIP and everything. But Major Winters hasn't shown up yet, and nobody's heard from him this morning, and I'm not doing shit else until somebody tells me what's going on."

"Huh." Domino turned to look at Z and Echo. "Are you saying something *happened* to Major Winters?"

Z leaned back against one of the crammed shelving units.

"No." Packard looked mortified by the fact anyone would even suggest such a thing. "I'm not saying something happened to the major." He stopped short, looked from one smiling pixie face to the other, then lurched to his feet and shouted, "What the fuck did you do to him?"

"Whoa, whoa, whoa." Domino calmly slid off the edge of the man's desk and lifted both hands. "Nobody said anything about *doing* anything to him."

"Perfect example of jumping to conclusions right there," Z added with a nod.

"Right?"

"I swear to god," Packard hissed, "if you don't tell me right now, I'll—"

"Give yourself an aneurism the way you're shouting like that," Domino interrupted. He looked the sergeant up and down and clicked his tongue. "Which is really saying something, you know? 'Cause I'm pretty sure that's only supposed to happen to the old humans. And you're so *young*."

Z shook her head in mock remorse. "Way too young."

When Packard didn't reply, Domino started questioning his assessment of the situation, then leaned in toward the sergeant and said, "You *are* pretty young, right? It's hard to tell with humans sometimes."

"Get out!" Packard thrust a finger toward the still-open office door. "If you don't have anything useful to tell me, leave me the hell alone so I can figure it out!"

"Hey, now," Z cooed. "Who said we don't have anything useful to tell you?"

"We're always useful, Sergeant."

"If you need help with this, you know you can come to us."

"I don't need help." Despite the fact he was still pointing at the door, the confident authority had started to drain from Packard's voice, mostly because he'd already put two and two together. When the pixies were on a roll, they didn't give a shit about following any orders an NCO barked at them, even if that NCO happened to be their *favorite*.

"Definitely not from you," he added, trying to remain firm. "When it's time for you to do something, somebody'll come find you. So get out."

After kicking herself away from the overstuffed shelf, Z pretended to pace across the tiny office. She tapped a finger against her lips in mock thoughtfulness. "Come to think of it, *we* haven't seen him in days, either."

"Great. I didn't ask—"

"So that begs the question. What kinda trouble did the major end up getting himself into?"

"Ooh!" Domino thrust his hand in the air but didn't wait for anyone to call on him. "Someone broke into his house and chained him to the radiator."

"Jesus Christ," Packard muttered. "For *what*?"

"I don't know. People just do that sometimes, right?"

"He hasn't been *sleeping* here since the end of our training, right?" Z mused. "No? That's what I thought. Maybe he got in a car accident on the way over. You know, a pileup on the freeway or whatever."

Domino snickered. "Doesn't sound very free."

"He could be in the hospital right now. Or in the back of a cop car."

"Ah. Right. The major goes rogue criminal."

Packard gaped at them. "What the hell is wrong with you?"

Z chuckled. "Well, that's a pretty long list, Sergeant."

"Just a *tad* longer than all the places Major Winters might be right now," Domino added. "And we're just getting started."

"Maybe he tried to pick up breakfast on his way in, and the breakfast place got held up by a couple robbers. With guns."

"Ooh, Z, that's good. Not as good as *us*, obviously, but it sounds like fun."

Z shrugged and kept pacing. "Or *maybe* it's more like a case of mistaken identity, you know? The major leaves this mountain to drive back to wherever he's been staying lately."

Domino shook his head. "Lucky bastard."

"And, sometime between then and now, he gets picked up by some other kind of top-level crime lord looking for his long-lost cousin. Major Winters fits the bill perfectly. That happens sometimes with humans, right, Sergeant? You guys get each other confused for other people and just end up making things even more confusing for yourselves."

"Ha." With a snort, Domino looked at his palms and examined his fingers. "After all the work you guys put into copying each other's fingerprints, you'd think it'd be easier to tell each other apart." He looked quickly up when he realized his sister had reached his side.

Echo leaned in to whisper in his ear, and he nodded sagely.

"She says a mountain lion could've gotten him whether or not he even likes hiking. Wait. There are mountain lions here? For real? That is so *awesome*."

"Why the fuck would he—" With a grunt, Packard closed his eyes and refrained from engaging any further in this ridiculous conversation. "In no universe anywhere, ever, is anything you just said considered even remotely helpful. The last thing I need is to listen to any more worst-case scenarios."

Domino cocked his head. "Well, how else are you gonna figure out what happened to him?"

"I wait for a fucking phone call. That's how." Packard pointed at the door again. "And if you assholes really have no idea where he is, then the best thing for you to do is to shut up, get out of my office, and stay out of my way until someone finds you with your next orders. Got it?"

The pixies just stared at him, waiting for the sergeant to say something else since he always did.

"That means now!"

Before the pixies had a chance to agree, ask more questions, or even have a rare moment of following orders, the obnoxious ring of Packard's desk phone filled the office.

Everyone looked at it, and the sergeant was the only one who didn't look disgusted. It rang again, and Domino cleared his throat. "You gonna get that?"

"Out!"

"Sergeant, you're looking stressed." Z headed toward the desk and reached for the phone. "I'm pretty good at answering phones and taking messages if you wanna, you know, sit back and chill out for a sec—"

Packard surprised them all by smacking her hand away from the phone and muttering, "Fuck off, Blue." He snatched the phone off the cradle and lifted it to his ear. "This is Sergeant Packard."

"Ho-*ho!*" Domino feigned surprise as he turned toward his sister and pointed in the sergeant's direction. "Look who's master of his realm."

Echo fixed her brother with a deadpan stare, then closed her eyes.

"What? Oh, come on. His realm's a *closet.*"

"Oh." Packard let out a massive sigh of relief and slumped into his office chair, then remembered the pixies and sat upright again. "I'm sorry to hear that, sir. No, everything's fine here. Just waiting for your—Yep. Uh-huh. Yes, sir, we'll be there. Got it."

He slammed the phone back down and shook a finger at them. "You little shits just got real lucky."

"You know who you're starting to sound like, right?" Domino shot the man a crooked smile. "I can tell you if you need a hint."

Packard ignored him but kept his hand firmly on the phone in its receiver. "You have twenty minutes to get your gear out of the bay and get your asses back here before we rendezvous with our transport out front."

"Out front?" Z's eyes widened. "Out front as in, in front of the *mountain?*"

"More importantly, *outside* it," Domino added. "Right?"

The sergeant sighed heavily and finally had to give up his attempt at being as much of a hardass as Major Winters was with these three new recruits. He slumped in his office chair and closed his eyes. "Just go do it."

"Oh, wait." Domino pointed at the phone. "That was *Major Winters* on the phone."

"Wow, Sergeant." Z spread her arms in disbelief. "Way to keep us in the loop. You should've told him hi from us."

"You can tell him yourself when we're outside in twenty minutes, okay? Just please, *please*, shut up and get the fuck out."

The three pixies stared at him, then Z chuckled and stuck her hands on her hips. "Aw."

Domino looked back and forth between them. "I mean, he *did* say please."

"So earnestly, too."

The only thing Packard felt he could do was close his eyes and pretend he was falling asleep since he just couldn't handle having to talk to them anymore. He silently counted the seconds and tried to fill his mind with all the things he'd be able to do again once this insane new group of OIP magicals was officially off to their new jobs and Packard himself was officially given another assignment.

He was so focused on those two things that he didn't notice when the pixies left his office until the room had been quiet for quite some time.

Too quiet.

Opening one eye, Packard scanned his tiny office for any sign of Z and her cousins, but there was none, not even the slightest sigh or poorly concealed giggle.

His heart lurched into his throat, and he sat bolt-upright in his chair, fervently looking for hints of pixie mischief. Everything seemed to be relatively in order, which could only mean the new recruits had left to get their things.

"Shit." Packard pushed himself out of the chair and headed briskly to the hall.

Someone had to go make sure the Army's three new winged soldiers didn't end up tearing the base down in the process of leaving it, hopefully for good.

CHAPTER SIXTEEN

"Well, tie me up and fuck me, Sally!" Domino proclaimed as he strolled across the grass, his arms uplifted toward the sunny blue sky and the morning sun.

Z snorted as she and Echo left the facility's exterior walls behind them. "I think you mean 'sideways.'"

"What?" He spun to face her and dropped his arms. "That doesn't even make sense."

"Neither did what *you* just said, but I'm glad you're feeling happy."

"Oh, yeah." Stretching his arms straight out to his sides, Domino took a deep breath of the crisp morning air, then sighed. "I'm definitely that."

The exit door clanged open and out stepped Sergeants Balsam and Kayley, with Packard bringing up the rear. Each carried a duffel bag of personal items slung over one shoulder.

Unfortunately, Packard was the only one who didn't see the pile of newly issued duffel bags Z and her cousins had dropped right outside the exit door. He took a deep breath to call them back, as the toe of his boot caught in one of the straps and almost sent him flying.

Balsam and Kayley turned to frown as he struggled to maintain balance, but neither one of them offered to help.

"Need a hand, Sergeant?" Z called.

All three sergeants fixed her with varying degrees of distrust, and she chuckled. "Whoops. I mean Sergeant *Packard*. Thought that was obvious."

"You stay right there." Kayley gave her a warning glare. "The only thing you need to worry about is getting into that transport vehicle and doing whatever the hell Major Winters tells you to do."

"And if everything goes the way it's supposed to," Balsam added, "we'll never have to see your magical asses again."

"Oh, I wouldn't count on that," Z replied.

Domino spread his arms again and shouted, "We're pixies, Sergeant. Nothing ever goes the way it's supposed to."

He and Z fell into a round of snickering, and even Echo offered a rare smile as Packard finished extricating himself from the pixies' luggage. They'd discarded it in exactly the right place to ensure *someone* would trip over it.

Sergeants Balsam and Kayley didn't find any of it very funny.

Where did all those guys go, anyway? Z wondered. *Not that I'd be sad never to see any of them again.*

"Come on!" Packard shouted before finally tugging his boot free. Then he chucked his duffel bag across the grass and glared at the pixies. "Come pick up your shit."

"You're closer," Z quipped.

"And you're gonna kill somebody pulling crap like that." Packard didn't have to say that he thought that someone might be him. Balsam and Kayley looked surprised to hear him say anything about it.

"Ugh." Rolling her eyes, Z stuck one hand on her hip and raised the other in a careless gesture. "There's always *something* ruining the fun, am I right?"

"Blue!"

"Woo. Sergeant." She flicked a finger at the three pixie-owned duffel bags, all of which illuminated in glowing bursts of deep-blue light before they raced over the tallest blades of grass and deposited themselves right at her feet. "Everything's gonna be okay. I promise."

"Just stop talking."

"And look at you, Sergeant." At this point, Domino had sidled up to Kayley's side without the NCO noticing, and now he stood only four feet away, inching closer.

"Nope." Kayley stared straight ahead, refusing to engage the pixies now just as he'd refused every other time they'd tried to goad him.

Domino looked the man up and down, then inched closer. "You seem tense. I mean, I know it's a sad day and everything, with the three of us leaving and the three of you…I don't know, being jobless after this, right?"

The sergeants shot the pixies incredulous stares.

"Shut your fucking mouth," Balsam barked.

"We are *not* losing our jobs," Packard muttered dejectedly. "If anything, we'll get a raise."

Echo shrank and took off in a streak of silver-gray light.

"Where's she going?" Balsam grumbled.

"Just stretching her wings," Z replied.

"Dammit, just because we're outside doesn't mean you freaks can just buzz around whenever you want."

Domino snickered. "We didn't have to be *outside* to do that."

"Private!" Kayley barked.

Echo, of course, didn't feel like listening to anybody. She was too enthralled with the feeling of the crisp, fresh air rushing over her wings and all the open space

The sergeants didn't like that one bit.

"Feet on the ground, Private!"

"If anyone sees you up there, you'll blow this whole thing wide open!"

"Don't make me open fire!"

Z snickered at that last one, and Echo paid no attention to the three NCOs shouting for her to quit flying around, quit jeopardizing the program, quit being a pixie. Of course, that only made the goth flitter even faster and higher, her silver-gray light trailing behind her like she was a giant firefly.

Domino stared from one sergeant to the next with wide eyes. He looked like he was about to burst out laughing but instead, he stepped closer to Sergeant Kayley and fixed the NCO with a healthy dose of concern. "Jeez. Army really wound you guys up *tight*, huh? You need to relax. How about a massage?"

"Don't fucking touch me," Kayley growled, batting Domino's hand away.

There was no telling how much more trouble Z and her cousins might have gotten themselves into if the low rumble of a large vehicle engine hadn't risen from the other side of the hill blocking the rest of their mountainside location from view. Shortly after, the vehicle itself barreled over that last hill with a sputtering roar and raced down the dirt road toward them.

"All right." Z pointed at the oncoming utility vehicle. "Is that our ride?"

Balsam and Kayley looked like they were about to be sick as the vehicle closed. Echo darted back and forth among the pine trees lining the open ground outside the facility.

"Private Thornbrook!" Kayley roared.

"Whoa, hey." Domino stepped away from him a wiggled a finger in his ear. "You don't have to yell so loud, Sergeant. I'm right here."

"I mean *that* one." Just as the NCO pointed up in the air at the orb of flickering silver-gray light that was Echo, the light disappeared. "Shit."

Domino giggled. "That's not her name. I mean, come on. Our parents weren't *that* sadistic."

"Are you fucking kidding me right now?"

"What? No." The copper pixie frowned at the sergeant, genuinely confused by the question. "Why would anyone name their kid—"

"Whatever her name is, get her back down here," Balsam barked.

"Wow. You hear that, Z? These fine sergeants have been escorting us all through the mountain for *weeks*, and they never took the time to learn our names."

Z sighed and shook her head. "Probably should've been first on your list, Sergeants."

"Listen," Packard chimed in as he stepped toward Z.

"Major Winters is in that vehicle, and if he sees there are three of us out here and only two of you, we're all screwed."

"Ha!" Domino pointed at the trees in the general direction of where his sister had disappeared. "She's already out here."

Z shielded her eyes with a hand and stared at the same spot, then shook her head. "Yeah, I don't think she's in a listening mood right now."

"Well, put her in one!"

They ran out of time because the vehicle carrying Major Winters was only a few meters away, spraying dirt and gravel as it bounced over the uneven road.

Z fought back another laugh. *Jeez. The way he's driving that thing, I'd say we're already screwed.*

When the vehicle showed no immediate signs of stopping or even slowing down, a blinding burst of silver light erupted twenty feet above the road. It shot straight down like a lightning bolt and crashed into the dirt in another burst of blinding light.

It was so blinding, that whoever happened to be behind the wheel slammed on the brakes and sent the vehicle fishtailing to an abrupt halt. Dirt and shredded grass sprayed in all directions.

Balsam and Packard shouted in surprise. A plume of fine dust rose from both behind the vehicle's rear wheels and just in front of the front bumper, illuminated by the pulse of silver light that almost looked like some kind of new explosive. When the silver light faded and the dust cleared, there stood Echo.

She landed just in front of the vehicle with her arms

folded, her all-black uniform, wings and hair stark against the clear blue horizon behind her. She was glaring straight into the vehicle's windshield at whoever happened to be sitting there. Her only reaction was to jerk her chin up at the vehicle's occupants and stand her ground.

"Holy shit." Sergeant Packard stared in horror.

"Get your ass back here, Private!" Sergeant Balsam barked.

"Really?" Domino leaned forward to stare at the man. "*That* looks more like she's in a listening mood than twenty seconds ago?"

The rumbling growl of the vehicle engine was the only sound as Major Winters flung open the driver-side door and leapt out. "What the fuck do you think you're doing, Private?"

Echo unfolded her arms to give her commander a slow, arcing wave with one hand.

"Jesus Christ." Winters spun toward his waiting sergeants. "Did she just come at me out of the fucking sky? Because it looked a hell of a lot like she just came at me out of the sky."

Z looked at the treetops where her cousin had been playing. "Then that's probably what happened."

"Shut up, Blue. I don't wanna hear a goddamn word out of your mouth."

Z and Domino exchanged an amused glance but didn't say anything as Major Winters took two furiously stumbling steps toward the NCOs and roared, "Sergeants!"

All three NCOs stood to attention.

"And not a single one of you has a goddamn thing to say about it?" Winters roared. "I asked you a question!"

For a moment, it seemed none of them was going to speak. Since Sergeant Kayley had the longest time in rank among them, he took it upon himself to answer. "She came from the sky, sir, yes."

"And what the *fuck* was an OIP soldier doing in the fucking *sky*, Sergeant Kayley?"

Beads of sweat formed on Kayley's forehead, but he somehow managed to stare straight ahead and keep a straight face when he swiftly replied, "She flew up there with her wings, sir."

"Her wings." Winters stepped aside to cast Echo a quick, scathing look, then returned his ire onto the sergeants who were particularly ill-equipped to keep pixies on the ground but were paying the price for that inability anyway. "I don't care if she turns into a fucking dragon, Sergeant. It's your job to keep your soldiers compliant and on the ground!"

"Yes, sir."

Domino snickered. "Turns into a dragon."

"Right?" Z murmured. "I'd pay to see that."

"I said shut it!" Winters thrust a trembling finger toward her but kept staring at the lined-up sergeants as if *they* were the problem. The sound of his heavy breathing joined the vehicle's rumbling engine as he tried to calm himself. He dropped his extended arm and growled. "Shit. We're on a timeline that wrapped up two goddamn hours ago. Sergeant Packard!"

"Sir." Packard looked relieved to have his commanding officer onsite again.

"Get these soldiers and their gear in the jeep." Winters patted down the front of his uniform shirt, then his sides pockets, frowning as he couldn't find what he was looking for.

With a frown, Packard looked at the pixies and nodded at the vehicle. "You heard the major."

"Nobody move!" Winters' self-pat-down grew in urgency, then he hissed and turned. "Damnit. Where are they?"

"Can I help you find something, Major?" Packard asked, moving to assist his commander.

Z snorted. "So helpful."

When she glanced at Balsam and Kayley to gauge their reactions, she found the sergeants sharing a knowing look between them. Balsam shrugged, and Kayley rolled his eyes.

Well, look at that. Something we can finally agree on.

Z was going to head over and strike up a friendly conversation, but Major Winters noticed.

"Whatever you're thinking about doing, Blue, don't."

Z stopped and smiled calmly, willing to let that one go because the major's current state of agitation was entertaining enough.

"Damnit, they were right here." Winters patted himself down again, then spun back toward the idling vehicle and the open driver-side door. "Worst morning of my life."

"These, sir?" Packard reached into the open vehicle and pulled out what looked like nothing more than strips of black cloth.

"Shit. Yeah. Those are for the Looney Toons over there. Go hand 'em out." The major stuck a thumb over his shoulder, then briskly tugged down the front of his uniform shirt and took a moment to compose himself while his back was still turned toward everyone else—except Echo.

When he noticed the goth was still standing there just in front of the vehicle's front bumper, Winters glared at her. "I got something on my face, Private?"

She didn't answer, so he rolled his eyes and let it go. "I swear on my mother's cats, if you don't step in line with the rest of the circus, I *will* run you over."

Echo raised an eyebrow at the front of the vehicle, then rolled her eyes and strode back toward the other pixies.

"Cats?" Packard looked up from the strips of cloth in his hands and frowned at his CO.

Winters clicked his tongue. "I'm pretty sure she loves those cats more than me. Go on."

Blinking in confusion, the young sergeant headed toward the pixies.

Balsam and Kayley smirked as Packard gingerly handed a strip of cloth to each of the pixies before stepping back to wait for whatever happened next.

"Hope none of you are afraid of the dark," Balsam chuckled.

Domino turned his piece of cloth over in his hand, snickered, and nodded at Echo. "Have you *met* my sister? What do you think?"

He paused to look at the NCOs, who looked way too happy about what was happening. "Why?"

"'Cause that's exactly where you're going," Kayley replied, smugly folding his arms.

Domino frowned, then looked up to scan the clear blue sky. "Huh. Looks pretty bright to me. Maybe you should get your eyes checked, Sergeant."

"Every one of you better be in the back of this vehicle with those blindfolds on in the next three minutes," Major Winters barked as he got back behind the wheel, "or so help me…"

"Blindfolds?" Z held the black strip of cloth out in front of her, then looked back at the vehicle and gestured toward the sergeants. "They didn't get theirs yet, Major."

"I wasn't talking to them." The driver-side door slammed shut, and Z and her cousins found themselves staring at three sergeants who looked far too keen about tossing them into the back.

CHAPTER SEVENTEEN

"Blindfolds," Z repeated. She glanced at the waiting vehicle. "Not gonna happen."

"Those are your orders." Sergeant Kayley took a step toward her. "Either *you* put it on, or we'll put it on for you."

"I'd like to see you try."

Domino sniffed tentatively at his blindfold, then pulled it away and wrinkled his nose. "These smell weird."

"Nobody gives a shit what you think they smell like, Private," Balsam added. "Put it on."

"And how, exactly, are you gonna make us do that, Sergeant?" Z folded her arms, the strip of black cloth dangling from one of her hands. "Because you're not capable of keeping your soldiers on the *ground*, either. No, really. Enlighten me."

Major Winters sounded the vehicle's horn, but the only person who reacted was Sergeant Packard, who started before deciding Kayley needed support. He headed for the vehicle's driver-side door. Everyone ignored him. Balsam and Kayley were trying to stare down three pixies.

Glaring at the sergeants, Echo took one end of the blindfold in each hand and tugged the strip taut with a loud snap.

Domino stuck his thumb out toward her. "What she said."

Winters rolled down his window just as Sergeant Packard stopped in front of it. He peered past the sergeant to yell, "What the hell's the holdup?"

"Couple of privates don't feel like following orders, Major," Kayley replied without taking his eyes off Z. "We'll take care of it."

She snickered. "You're doing a great job."

"Blue!" Winters barked. "Put it on!"

Domino whirled toward the vehicle and shouted, "Are you serious?"

"As a heart attack. Let's go!"

"I thought we were US soldiers, Major," Z called, still unwilling to break her staring contest with Sergeant Kayley, "But I'm having a hard time figuring out why you'd wanna do *this* to your own soldiers."

The major sighed and dipped his head, then shifted in his seat, stuck his head out the window, and put more force behind his next words. "You clowns are heading off to your next assignment, and this was part of the agreement to get you there. Now put on the fucking blindfold and move it!"

With an exaggerated groan, Z took the lead and lifted the black blindfold over her face before tying the whole thing on in one swift movement.

"That's a good little bug," Kayley muttered. "Now get your gear and get in the vehicle."

Domino had almost pressed the blindfold to his face

but lowered it and clicked his tongue. "Well, which one is it, Sergeant? You want us to get our stuff or get in the truck?"

"Both. Figure it out." Then Kayley grabbed Z by her upper arm to lead her toward the back of the idling vehicle.

She didn't put up a fight, but she did raise her other hand and, with a flick of her fingers, sent a streak of deep-blue light hurtling across the grass toward her new duffel bag carrying her few personal effects.

Balsam jumped out of the way, then watched as the blue-haired pixie's duffel bag surrounded with blue light darted off the ground and zipped toward the rear hatch of the vehicle that Sergeant Packard had just opened.

"Sergeant Kayley," Balsam warned, but he was already too late.

Z's duffel bag hit Kayley in the back of the head, glanced off his shoulder, and spun wildly through the air until it thumped onto the floor of the vehicle's interior with a jingle of silver buckles and zippers.

"What the—" Kayley didn't know *where* to look for the source of the projectile luggage, but he saw the smirk on Z's lips as he hauled her along. "Very cute."

"Hey, you said to figure it out. And a pixie *lives* outside the box, Sergeant." She didn't struggle as he jerked her toward the back of the vehicle and told her when to step inside.

Sergeant Packard's eyes widened as he realized Domino and Echo were following Z's example.

"Sergeant Kayley," he muttered as the other sergeant turned away from the open back hatch of the vehicle. "You might wanna get out of the—"

One duffel bag hit Kayley on the shoulder in an explosion of silver light before thumping down in the vehicle at Z's feet. It was immediately followed by a second bag surrounded by flickering copper light, which Kayley had the presence of mind to duck.

"How'd we do, Z?" Domino shouted as Sergeant Balsam grabbed him by the arm and hauled him toward the vehicle.

"Bullseye!"

"Excellent."

No one stood beside Echo to escort her, and no one seemed to care when she walked over to join her cousins. She waited silently for the sergeants to hop into the vehicle with their two passengers so she could get in herself.

"Hurry it up," Kayley grumbled, then noticed Echo standing outside. *Without* her blindfold already tied around her head like the others.

Domino chuckled. "Nothing wrong with her aim, Sergeant."

Packard shook his head and gestured to the back of the vehicle. "Just go already."

Echo silently complied, settling onto the bench beside her brother.

Packard wished there was something he could say to help dampen the tension, but the glares from the other sergeants made it impossible to think of anything. He sighed and shut the vehicle's rear hatch before joining Major Winters up front.

A loud, grating squeal rose from the vehicle's front. Then they lurched into a U-turn before taking off back down the road toward their new assignments.

For a blissful ninety seconds, the back of the vehicle was silent. Balsam and Kayley stared at the three blindfolded pixies sitting opposite, knowing the recruits were bound to start something.

Once the dirt road gave way to asphalt, Domino took a deep breath, let it out, and rolled his shoulders back. "Seems kinda weird that covering our faces with stinky cloth is an actual requirement for giving us jobs."

Balsam pressed his lips together and shook his head. "You really think anybody trusts you enough to let you see exactly how to get to and from an Army base?"

"Isn't that what maps are for?" Z asked.

"Not every part of a base is on a map," Kayley grumbled. "Most of where we've been for the last six weeks sure as hell isn't."

"But it's so *beautiful* out here," Domino added, turning his head back and forth as if he were looking through the windows behind them.

"Just stop talking."

For a few more minutes, the pixies did. Then Z scooted forward in excitement. "Ooh. Dom. They have a zoo here."

"No way." Her cousin grinned beneath his blindfold. "We should totally check that out. Hey, Sergeant Kayley. Do we ever get time off to go to the zoo?"

Kayley sneered back at him. "You'd fit right in there, wouldn't you?"

"Aw, thank you." The vehicle went over a few more bumps making a slow turn before picking up speed, then Domino chuckled. "Z, we should remember this spot."

"Why's that?"

"'Cause I've always wanted to try mountain beer. Breweries everywhere. Doesn't the elevation get you super sloshed?"

"That's not a bad idea. What do you think, Echo?"

The goth shrugged.

Neither of the others turned to look at her but kept on talking as if they could see her.

"Looks like she's in," Z added.

"All right." Domino pumped his fists on either side of his head. "We got ourselves a plan. Whenever the bosses decide to give us time off to enjoy this beautiful city of... Wait, what's it called again?"

"Colorado Springs."

"How do you know?"

Z nodded at the window. "It was on a sign."

"Nice."

Sergeants Balsam and Kayley realized something wasn't quite right. The pixies were talking about things that were outside the vehicle despite both of them being blindfolded.

"Hey, check it out. That train goes all the way up the mountain."

"You ever ride a train up a mountain before, Sergeant Balsam?"

"Man, the skyline right there. Am I right? Bet that makes for a great sunset."

It didn't take long for the two sergeants to move past confused to disbelieving. As Domino and Z kept shouting out landmarks, restaurants, and sights they couldn't possibly see, Balsam had to turn and double-check their surroundings himself.

"How the fuck are they doing this?" he whispered.

"Doing what?" Domino asked happily, clasping his hands in his lap.

Kayley waved a hand back and forth in front of Echo's blindfolded face. She waited just long enough to let him feel comfortable before snapping at him like a rabid dog.

"Shit!" He whipped his hand back, whacked his elbow against the vehicle wall, then scowled at the pixies while trying not to nurse his arm.

Z and Domino burst out laughing, and Echo sat back against the wall with a smirk.

"They've been here before," Kayley said with a grunt. "That's all this is."

"What, in Colorado Springs?" Z shook her head. "First time. A whole six weeks locked up inside a mountain, and we're just getting to see the world again."

Domino scrunched his shoulders. "It's so *exciting*."

"Don't get me wrong, it would've been nice to get a more of a hands-on feel for the place, but I'm guessing the Army doesn't do guided tours."

Both sergeants shook their heads and pressed their backs firmly against the walls. They had no choice but to listen to the cousins babble about what they couldn't possibly see. Up front, Major Winters and Sergeant Packard didn't hear a thing.

The vehicle finally slowed to a crawl, then stopped.

"Ooh," Domino said. "Are we there yet?"

Balsam and Kayley exchanged a murderous look but didn't reply.

Over the rumbling engine, they heard good-natured greetings. Z and her cousins waited quietly, biding their time for the next fun opportunity to present itself.

One voice rose above the others. "Good morning, Major. Sorry to bother you about this now."

"Don't be. What's going on?"

"Sergeant Major McDonald at Gate Four just radioed to tell me they were expecting you on post way out there. You're usually pretty good about getting where you need to be, so I just want to make sure everything's all right, sir."

"Just a change of plans, Sergeant. Had to pivot a little, but we'll end up where we need to be."

"Yes, sir, I get it. I'll let him know you're heading that way." There was another pause. Then the soldier cleared his throat. "I'm, uh, sorry to ask, Major, but—"

"You want my ID, too, is that it?" Winters replied glumly. "Here you go, Packard. That's yours. Actually, Sergeant…"

"Henkle, sir."

"Sergeant Henkle. I ran into a SNAFU with that ID, which is partially the cause of that pivot this morning. It's being taken care of."

"Understood, sir."

At the mention of Major Winters' ID SNAFU, Z and her cousins snickered.

A soldier knocked on the outside of the rear window and waved for everyone to show their identification as well. The sergeants slapped their IDs up against the window and glared at their pixie subordinates.

The soldier nodded, then paused when he saw a weird blue shimmer inside the vehicle. Frowning, he cupped his hands around his eyes for a better look through the window and saw the three pixies grinning at him.

"Going through a different kind of intake with those

three," Winters called from the front. "I'm vouching for 'em."

"Yes, sir. Have a good one."

The vehicle rolled gently through the gate.

"You hear that, Dom?" Z elbowed her cousin in the ribs. "He's *vouching* for us."

"Right? And it's not even someone's birthday. Still a sweet thing to say, though."

CHAPTER EIGHTEEN

When Major Winters parked at their final destination, he still had to give himself a moment to calm down.

That's not gonna fly twice with no ID. It's like the universe decided to pile every piece of shit on me today.

"Everything okay, sir?" Packard asked.

"Peachy." Winters shut off the engine and got out to address the three OIP soldiers.

Rounding the back of the vehicle, he found Sergeants Balsam and Kayley standing beside the open rear hatch. The pixies remained in the back, lined up neatly on the bench with their blindfolds on.

"I'm not giving y'all orders for every little thing. What the hell're y'all waitin' for?"

Domino leaned forward. "Oh, *hi*, Major. That was a fun little ride."

"Little worried about security, though," Z added, equally as blindfolded. "Looked like those boys at the gate could really use an extra hand, know what I mean? Lotta slack needs to be picked up if the Army's gonna succeed at keeping out all the people it wants to keep out."

Domino nodded. "I'll second that."

Winters glared at them, one eye twitching, then he sniffed and muttered, "Get the hell out here and keep up. We ain't done yet."

"Whew! Finally!" With a whoop, the copper pixie leapt to his feet and out of the vehicle. His boots clapped down on smooth concrete, and he spread his arms. "We're *here*!"

"Take that thing off," Kayley grumbled.

Z and Echo followed, and all three pixies removed their blindfolds and took a good look around using their eyes instead of the magic they'd been using on the trip.

"Nice place." Z nodded, sizing up the area sectioned off for the next phase of the Oriceran Integration Program. "Is this all yours, Major?"

"Could use a more personal touch if you ask me," Domino added.

They caught up with Winters, who looked at them before pausing. "Where's your stuff?"

"In the car."

"For the love of—" Winters inhaled deeply, then gestured at the vehicle. "Go get it."

"You just told us to keep up, Major," Z clarified. "So... Not really sure how we're supposed to do both."

The man's eyes bulged. "Then figure it out."

As soon as the words left his lips, Kayley called from the back of the open vehicle, "I'll handle it, sir."

Winters didn't argue, so the sergeant immediately reached into the back to grab three pixie duffel bags, cursing under his breath the whole time. Carrying three duffel bags into the next building seemed like a better deal than getting smacked in the back of the head with them.

The whole team headed toward a small, squat building located outside a gated area that seemed to stretch on forever. The pixies studied the structure, then Z let out a noncommittal hum. "Meh. Honestly, I thought it'd be bigger."

Domino snickered. "That's what *she* said."

Winters stopped at the front door of the squat concrete building, then turned to face everyone else. "Sergeant Packard, you're with us. Sergeants Balsam and Kayley, go get that vehicle back to the garage and take the rest of the day off. You'll hear from me in the morning."

"Thank you, sir."

The sergeants turned to leave, and Z tossed her blindfold toward them. "Here. Take these with you, will ya?"

The black strip of cloth flopped against Balsam's face, and he soon had all three of them dangling over his arm. He stopped to glare at the pixies, but they were following Major Winters into the building, duffel bags slung over their shoulders.

"We should fucking burn those things," Kayley muttered.

"You're telling me." Balsam held the blindfolds out by the tips of his fingers and followed suit. After a quick glance around to make sure no one was watching, he lifted one to his eyes to test its integrity, then he quickly whipped it back down and stalked after his fellow NCO, shaking his head.

The building Winters and the pixies entered was yet another security checkpoint, something which became clear when they were stopped inside the first door, then again halfway between the first and the second, and again both before *and* after they were led through that second door and into a large waiting room.

Apparently, this particular area of the Army base had a much higher level of security, judging by the fact that each stop beside each new door lasted at least ten minutes. Every soldier on duty asked for Winters' ID card, which he couldn't hand over since he didn't have it.

After that came radio calls, systems' checks, running the major's fingerprints, and well-meaning suggestions for Winters to get that fixed as soon as possible so he wouldn't have to go through this every time he needed access.

At first, the man took it in stride, but after going through the same routine a second time, he stopped telling them that getting a new ID was why he was here.

After that, he responded to all questions with flat one-word answers, clenching his jaw and sighing and sounding like Echo.

As they were waiting for the final guard to clear Winters and his recruits—none of whom had IDs—the pixies could no longer keep themselves from laughing.

"You're doing *great*, Major," Domino said, giving him a thumbs-up.

Z nodded. "Honestly, I've never seen someone answer the same questions over and over again with *exactly* the same answers every time. There's no cracking a hole in *your* story, that's for sure."

"Nobody asked for your opinions," he retorted.

Then the soldier in charge of this particular round of security questions turned his head away from his radio and nodded at them. "Thanks for your patience, Major. You're all clear. And if you wanna grab yourself a new ID while you're here, Intake's right—"

"I know where it is."

"Yes, sir."

Winters stalked toward one of the long desks at the far side of the room. The pixies took their time following and studied what the inside of an aboveground Army facility looked like.

The soldier who'd let them in couldn't stop staring at their wings. He wasn't the only one, either. Everyone they passed had also seemed confused by Echo's all-black OCPs and boots, but no one was willing to say anything about it near Major Winters.

He must be a pretty big deal around here, then. Big enough for everybody to just let him through the next gate without an actual ID on him.

"Nah, you know what?" Domino shoved his hands into his pockets. "I'm gonna go ahead and say the last place was cooler."

"And that's not just because it was in a mountain?"

"I mean, that's part of it, yeah. But everything here looks…drab and dirty."

Echo scuffed her foot along the carpeted floor, then she leaned toward her brother and whispered in his ear.

"As old as the major?" Domino shrugged. "Yeah, probably. I don't know. We could ask him."

They didn't have a chance, however, because Major Winters stopped at the desk for a brief conversation with the support staff there. He and the other soldier spoke in hushed tones, and the soldier had a hard time maintaining eye contact with his superior when there were three soldiers standing behind Winters, all with different-colored wings.

"Understood, sir," the guy said, nodding curtly. "We can get started now if you want."

"Yep. If you need anything else, Sergeant Packard here can get it for you. I'm stepping out for a minute." Before he did, though, Winters approached the pixies, scanning the rest of the mostly empty waiting room. He stopped uncomfortably close to his three new recruits and murmured, "This is not the last place. And we aren't exactly where we need to be, so I'm giving y'all one warning. Step out of line, and I'll put every single resource I have into calling that old gnome down on your asses, understand?"

Z and her cousins nodded, which seemed to satisfy him enough to drop the topic and head for the restroom. Z stopped him, however, when she added, "Didn't he say you wouldn't be able to get ahold of him?"

Domino pointed at her and nodded.

Winters scanned the rest of the lobby. "How do you think I got him to consult for the Army?" To accentuate his point, he flicked his gaze down to meet hers, narrowed his eyes, then stepped past her to take care of business.

Z stood perfectly still and grinned.

"Whoa-ho-ho." Domino clapped his hands together and shook them out as if they'd caught fire. "The major's puttin' on his big-boy boots now."

"Well, he's back on his home turf, right? Makes sense."

"Oh, boy." Domino rubbed his hands together and swept his gaze around the room. "I can't *wait* to get our hands on the turf."

Z and Echo frowned at him, but he was too excited to realize he'd used a phrase neither magicals nor humans would understand.

"Privates," Packard called from the desk before waving the pixies toward him.

Domino giggled. "You sure you wanna be shouting something like that out in public, Sergeant?"

The soldier behind the desk cocked his head, and Sergeant Packard knew he'd have to smooth things between new privates and the regulars around them.

Z and her cousins pretended not to notice and enjoyed the attention.

"You're getting your IDs," Packard told them. "Officially. So get over here and talk to Corporal Townsend."

"Oh, boy!" Domino rubbed his hands together and led the way. "Real IDs? With glamor shots and everything?"

Townsend looked worried. "Sergeant?"

"Feel free to ignore ninety percent of what they say, Corporal." Packard gave him what was supposed to be a reassuring nod, then gave the pixies a stern look.

"Well, they're, uh..." Corporal Townsend looked from the magicals to Sergeant Packard. "They're close to regular IDs, I guess, with a few extra modifications."

"Lemme guess," Z started. "They can fly."

"Ooh. They change faces on the front!" Domino added.

"Conjure food?"

"Broadcast whale calls!"

Echo whispered in her brother's ear.

He leaned away from her in surprise, then shrugged. " I have no idea why anyone would wanna start slitting throats with their own ID card, but that's what she said."

"Um…" Townsend clearly couldn't think of anything to say to that.

"I know it sounds like it," Packard murmured, "but that wasn't a threat. Trust me."

"Okay." The corporal puffed out a sigh, then continued with his original spiel. "Look, I don't know about all that other shit you guys just said, but your ID cards need a picture. So who's going first?"

Without even having to think about it, Z and Echo both shoved Domino forward between them. He stumbled under the force, slammed his hands down on the edge of Townsend's desk, and grinned. "Always."

CHAPTER NINETEEN

The pixies treated the process of getting their official Army ID cards as if it were an all-expenses-paid shopping spree in New York—which they *had* done before, but only because it had been funded by one of their jobs with Calinda.

It was a lot less glamorous this time, but that didn't stop them from having fun. It started with their ID photos. Sergeant Packard tried not to draw even more attention to the odd situation when he snapped at the pixies to take it seriously.

Domino went through five different rounds of snapshot seconds before Packard and Townsend finally gave up on the redoes. Z only asked once to redo hers, and Echo clearly didn't care one way or the other what her photo looked like.

Corporal Townsend focused on getting them their required clearance levels, documentation, badges, ID cards, and everything else they needed. As he did, Z and her cousins bombarded him with questions that had everything and nothing to do with why they were there.

"Does anybody else know about this part of the base?"

"You ever seen a pixie before?"

"How many times does someone have to be asked the same question before they're considered legit?"

"Is Major Winters the Big Boss of the Army or just, like, the Slightly Smaller Boss?"

"Want me to make your pencils fly? I can do it."

"How much of this place do we get to explore all on our own?"

Townsend did his best to both pay attention to his job and not make the curious new recruits feel snubbed or ignored when he couldn't answer their questions. Sergeant Packard neither stepped in to help nor told the pixies to cut it out. For once, he wasn't the object of their attention, and he wasn't going to change that.

Finally, the card printer spat out three perfectly crafted Army IDs. Corporal Townsend used the opportunity to interrupt the barrage of questions by lifting a finger toward the pixies and swiveling in his chair. "Hold on just a second. I think these are ready."

"Yes!" Domino pumped a fist at his side, and the pixies accepted their new IDs as if they were being given tiny, precious, extremely fragile little critters—with both hands cupped together and enormous smiles on their faces.

"This might be the best day of my life," Domino murmured.

"Definitely the best day of this week," Z added.

"A little heads-up." Townsend scooted his chair close to the desk and nodded at the IDs in question. "We had to work around a few protocols for these, obviously. I mean, I, uh, you guys don't *have* fingerprints, right?"

Domino scoffed. "Where'd you hear something crazy like that?"

Too late, Townsend realized his mistake in looking at Sergeant Packard.

"Sergeant Packard," Z said in mock consternation. "You like us so much that you've been telling everybody our secrets, huh?"

"That's not what I've been doing," the sergeant replied curtly, his previous aloofness gone. "And it's not a secret."

"Because it's totally wrong." Z leaned toward Townsend and nodded. "We *do* have fingerprints. Just not the kind that ends up printing anything."

"They move." Domino wiggled his fingers in a demonstration. Beside him, Echo lifted a hand to do the same.

"Right." The corporal cleared his throat. "Anyway, we can't fingerprint you, and it's not like we can just stick a biometric scanner onto every door and lock, right?" He snickered at his joke but quickly stopped when no one else joined him. "So those are basically your keys to get into everything. You need them. All the time. Might as well just glue 'em to your body, you know?"

"*Don't* do that," Packard warned. "He was being sarcastic."

"Obviously." Domino turned away from the desk to gaze lovingly at his ID's photograph.

"Yeah," Z added. "We don't have any glue."

As Townsend looked at Packard, Major Winters stormed back into the waiting room. "Well, I'll be damned.

Y'all somehow managed not to burn the place down in the first five minutes."

"Wait." Domino gestured between himself and the major. "Is that what you *wanted* us to do?"

"Don't. Those the IDs?"

"Fresh off the ID-print-a-ma-jigger," Z replied. "They look *good*, Major. Wanna see?"

"Nope. I already gotta look at y'all's faces enough as it is. How about getting me one of the same, Corporal?"

Townsend blinked furiously at the major. "Sir?"

"Nothing fancy like all that crap." Winters gestured toward the pixies' new ID cards. "Just a regular old replacement."

"Not a problem, sir."

Winters stood behind the necessary white line and didn't change his expression while the corporal took his picture for a replacement ID. "Great. Go ahead and send that up to my office when it's all finished. 'Preciate it. Sergeant Packard, I haven't had my second or even my first damn cup of coffee today."

"I can tell, sir," Packard muttered.

"And now you can tell where there's a pot of coffee in this building 'cause I know it exists. Now I've got a meeting with the other head honcho around here, and I'm already way too fucking late."

"Yes, sir." All Packard had to do was raise an eyebrow at Townsend for the corporal to subtly point him in the direction of the closest breakroom.

While the sergeant took off in one direction, Winters turned to head in the other but paused. Then he turned back to face Z and her cousins. "No, I didn't forget about y'all. Take a seat. Hang tight. Don't fuck anything up." He pointed at the row of chairs along the far wall and raised his eyebrows in warning. Without another word, the major turned fully around again and hurried off for his overdue meeting.

"The *other* head honcho?" Domino squinted after the major as he, Z, and Echo sat where they were told. "How does that work, then? Some kinda timeshare or something?"

"Dual custody," Z murmured. She took a moment to study her brand-new ID, knowing Corporal Townsend was watching them warily.

Official Army soldiers now. We got the cards to prove it and everything. Not nearly as cool as it sounds.

"Hot damn, I look good." Domino flipped his card around to show them his sixth and final photo. "Right?"

"Oh, yeah. You sure did put up a hell of a pucker."

"*Thank* you."

Z showed him hers while he held his out to trade with Echo.

"Oh, wow." Domino nodded. "Okay. So you went with anime-shimmer vibes."

"Okay, fine. Admittedly, I could've toned it down on the cheesy grin and glistening eyes." Z laughed and flicked her ID with a finger. "But that's a good-looking pixie in uniform right there. Echo, let's see yours."

Domino switched ID cards with his sister, then brought Echo's front and center for all of them to study.

"Holy shit."

"That's, uh, well…"

"So you're either taking a dump, stepping on a cactus, or…"

"Snarling at the local dogs to mark your territory," Z finished.

"Damn." Domino tilted his head to study the image from a different angle, then nodded. "That's pretty accurate. Good work."

He returned his sister's ID, and she did the same. Then the pixies were left alone with their first-ever pictures, new official badges, and nothing to do but wait in a different place.

Corporal Townsend finished typing, then rolled away from the desk and stood.

"Where ya goin', Corporal?" Z asked.

The man froze, tried to pretend he hadn't heard her, then realized there was no way they could have missed his reaction. "I gotta go check on something."

"Hey, want us to come with?" Domino asked.

"Nope. No. Definitely not. You just…stay there. I'll be right back." Townsend hesitated, expecting the pixies to argue or ask him some more ridiculous questions. When they didn't, he nodded to himself and hurried off to go take care of whatever he had to take care of.

As soon as he disappeared down the hallway off the main waiting room, the ID printer whirred, printing one final laminated card.

"Ooh, hey." Domino leaned forward to snatch a magazine from a small table beside the chairs, crossed one leg over the opposite knee and opened it. "Think there's anything good in here?"

Echo clicked her tongue and didn't say anything, but

she did lean slightly toward her brother for a look at the pictures.

Z tapped her boot on the floor, tired of waiting and tired of being told to do nothing. Even her cousins were too busy to notice anything she might or might not have done. She stood, clasped her hands behind her back, and walked down the waiting room, pretending to study the framed certificates and printed Army slogans hanging on the walls. The waiting room was emptier than when they'd first arrived, and there was no one to monitor a lone pixie walking back and forth, let alone all three of them.

In a burst of blue light, Z darted into her two-inch size, zipped across the room toward Townsend's desk, and resumed human size next to the card printer. If anyone had seen her, they would have noticed something wasn't quite right with the blue-haired soldier.

Nobody saw her snatch the new ID card with Major Winters' scowling face on it and deposit it in her side pocket. Nobody saw her lean toward Townsend's computer, click around a few times with the mouse, and casually step away again, either.

For as big as they are on security around here, it's shit on the inside. Guess the Army just never had a soldier it didn't trust until now.

Smirking, Z started to turn away from the desk, but a slightly familiar sensation stopped her.

It was the same thing she'd felt out in the woods before Calinda's gang had been rounded up by Alpha Team and the gnome. It wasn't exactly mind-reading or exactly feeling others' emotions, but something in between.

She recognized who the emotions and intentions

belonged to since they had Major Winters written all over them.

Why the hell am I feeling this now?

Looking around, she saw a small window in the waiting room wall, to the left behind Corporal Townsend's desk. Anyone looking through it wouldn't have seen the corporal working on his computer, but when Z looked out, she could see through to the other side.

There was Winters. He was standing with his arms folded and speaking in low tones to someone she couldn't see. The man looked like he usually did; he had a tight frown and pursed lips, and looked grumpy. Anyone else would have found it impossible to know what the man was thinking, but for Z, his intentions were perfectly clear.

Fix this giant mess. Gotta prove myself. Don't lose your shit.

Frowning, Z leaned away from the window and turned to eye the waiting room. It was still fairly empty, and the final soldier acting as security just inside the entrance seemed perfectly happy scrolling through his phone like everything was just fine around here.

Jeez. Looks like I'm the only one picking up on this. And the major's a serious bummer today.

She walked casually back to her cousins, who were still engrossed in flipping through magazine pages without reading a single one. They didn't notice when Z plopped down next to Domino. "You guys feeling anything weird in here right now?"

"Yeah, yeah," Domino muttered as Echo turned the page for him. "Totally."

"Dom."

"Huh?" He lifted his head, and a frown crossed his features. "What's up?"

"I thought I felt something in here a minute ago." Z forced herself not to look at the window behind Townsend's desk because that would give her away. "You guys aren't picking up on it?"

"What, like a tickle?" Her cousin turned another page. "Maybe it's indigestion."

Echo raised her eyebrows and clapped a hand over her stomach.

"Oh, yeah. Or hunger." Pursing his lips, Domino scanned the waiting room. "Still haven't had breakfast. Maybe Sergeant Packard'll bring us a few snacks."

"Yeah. Maybe." Z sat back in her chair and pretended to be perfectly content with sitting there and doing zilch, but her mind just wouldn't let go of the strange feeling that was already starting to fade.

She'd thought it had just been a fluke when she'd felt the intentions of Alpha Team during the raid in the woods. It had just seemed like an odd reflex, some kind of protective mechanism letting her sense danger but not giving her time to prepare for it.

This time, there was no immediate danger to her or her cousins. They were safe in a highly secured area of the base, surrounded by soldiers and guards and humans who all seemed confident in their ability to handle whatever came their way, and it wasn't like Major Winters was going to murder them when he needed to prove the OIP program worked.

Obviously, her strange ability to feel a human's intentions didn't have anything to do with self-preservation this time.

Winters was in the woods that night too, though. Oh, man. I really hope this isn't from some kinda weird special connection my magic wants to have with the guy. He's no fun. So why am I feeling all this now?

CHAPTER TWENTY

It didn't take long for Major Winters to return. Just as he reemerged from the hallway at one end of the waiting room, Sergeant Packard appeared at the other. He walked slowly, precariously balancing two cups of coffee and a box of donuts in his hands while trying to watch where he was going.

Domino sniffed at the air, then turned to Z. "There's our breakfast."

Winters and Packard converged where Z and her cousins were waiting. Both looked skeptical that the magical recruits had done nothing but sit there as they'd been told.

The major squinted at them, but whatever he might have said was waylaid by Sergeant Packard shoving a cup of coffee in his face.

"Coffee, sir."

"Thanks." Winters took a moment to drink, grimaced, then looked Packard up and down. "What's in the box?"

"Donuts, sir."

"Huh. Good thinking." The major fiddled with the box's lid, apparently oblivious to his sergeant's struggle to balance the box and his cup of coffee.

Winters pulled out a massive donut covered in powdered sugar and jammed it into his mouth. As he chewed, he stared at Z and her cousins, all of whom looked at him to see what they were going to end up doing next.

"Time to get y'all situated," he said through his mouthful and jerked his head toward the hallway from which he'd just entered. "Let's go."

After that, he turned to stalk back down the hall, alternating between donut bites and sips of coffee.

Z and her cousins stood, shouldered their bags, and turned toward Sergeant Packard.

"That was super thoughtful of you, Sergeant," Z said with a beaming smile.

He blinked at her in confusion. "What?"

Before he could put two and two together, she'd plunged her hand into the box of donuts and grabbed one covered in chocolate frosting and sprinkles. "Nice."

"Ooh, yeah." Domino wiggled his fingers over the box. "Don't mind if I do," then his hand darted in and came back out with his selected breakfast snack.

Packard staggered under the assault of hands taking the food he'd found while trying not to spill his coffee. "That's not—"

"There's a reason why you're our favorite," Domino interrupted, thumping the sergeant's shoulder and leaving a smear of cinnamon-sugar grains.

Packard had been going to turn away, but a warning glare from Echo made him freeze.

She stared at him as she took one donut, then a second. She lifted the treats toward him in a silent toast, pivoted, and followed the other pixies.

Blinking in surprise and confusion, Packard opened his mouth to call after the magicals and Major Winters, who were heading somewhere else in the facility, but no sound emerged. He glanced at the open donut box and gave a dejected sigh.

As he followed his commanding officer, Packard stopped beside Townsend's desk and dumped the empty donut box in the trash.

It came as no surprise that Major Winters led the pixies into yet another empty room. Z and her cousins dumped their bags on the floor and sized up the space.

"Not really as homey as the last place, Major," Z said before taking another bite from her donut.

"Yeah," Domino added, folding his arms. "And where are the beds?"

"The hell're you talking about?" Winters grumbled.

"You said we were getting situated."

The man stared, then gestured at the table in the center of the room. "Have a seat."

The pixies did as instructed. Domino propped his elbows on the table and propped his chin up in both hands. "Should've brought a bed."

"This ain't your damn room, Private. This is where y'all get your jobs."

"*Oh.*" The copper pixie sat up. "But they'll have beds

there, right?"

Z couldn't help a small smile as the major tried to reign in his irritation under this new barrage of questions, then a new thought occurred to her.

What if I can read his mind? Wouldn't hurt to know what's coming next, right?

While Winters reached toward the stack of printed packets waiting for them, Z narrowed her eyes and watched him intently, trying for that sensation of *knowing* what he intended to do with them next.

Winters tossed a packet in front of each pixie, pausing as his gaze settled on Z. "What's wrong with you?"

"Me? Nothing, Major." She narrowed her eyes further, imagining herself prying into his head to pull out his thoughts. "I'm just…excited."

His frown deepened as he studied her. "Well, be excited without staring at me like that. You're creeping me out."

Z sighed and sat back in her chair. *Guess not.*

Domino burst out laughing. "If *that* creeps you out, Major, wait 'til you see—"

"Not interested," Winters snapped. He nodded at the packets and began explaining what the next step in the pixies' Army agreement entailed. "Y'all had your evaluations the other day, and Dr. Goldbloom got back to me with her recommendation for your new jobs. I'm taking her at her word here, which is why we're posting you here as 31Es."

"Oh, cool." Domino nodded vigorously. "Yeah, okay. 31E."

He stopped and cocked his head. "What's that?"

Winters sighed heavily and rubbed his face. He seemed

incapable of looking any of them in the eye as he explained. "I can't for the life of me figure out why the hell the woman recommended *this* as a starting place for you, but that's what we're going with. After that, we'll just have to wait and see."

"So you made up a brand-new job?" Z asked. "Just for us?"

"What? No. I said 31E."

"Which is?"

The man looked uncomfortable. "Military police."

The room fell silent as the news sank in, then Domino slapped a hand on the table and grinned. "Yes!"

"Military police," Z mused, mulling over what that meant. "I like the sound of that."

"Do we get badges?" Domino asked.

Winters stared blankly at him. "I don't know."

"What about pistols?"

"Handcuffs?"

"Ooh! What about those weird little guns that make people jerk around on the ground when you shoot 'em?"

"Lasers," Domino clarified incorrectly.

"You sure?" Z asked.

"Totally. Laser guns. Major, do we get to carry around lasers in a holster?" The copper pixie lifted both hands above the table and aimed two finger guns at his commander.

Winters shook his head. "Nobody's giving you tasers until you've done the required training."

"Tasers?" Domino leaned away, looking insulted. "What's *that*?"

Echo leaned sideways to whisper in her brother's ear.

"Oh, yeah. That's good! She says what about horses?"

"Horses? Why the fuck?" The major frowned. "That's not even close. You obviously have no damn clue what military police even means."

Domino shrugged. "We know police, sure."

"Trust us, Major," Z added as she folded her arms with a smug smile. "We've spent plenty of time running from cops. We know all about it."

"And you can count on us to be better, faster, and stronger than *all* of them!"

"Jesus." Winters pinched the bridge of his nose while the pixies grinned at each other and exchanged high-fives. He took another sip of his coffee, grimaced, and pushed on. "This isn't a party, Privates. This is serious stuff."

"Totally serious."

"The most serious."

"We're nothing but serious, Major."

Now Z and Domino stared back with the exact same deadpan expression Echo always wore. The effect of being eyed like that by all three pixies made Winters' gut churn.

"Training comes first," he told them. "MPs are responsible for keeping the peace, area damage control, critical site security, convoy and personnel escorts, and maintaining law and order wherever they're stationed. In a nutshell."

"Ooh, buddy!" Domino rubbed his hands together.

"Hold on." Z pointed at the major. "Does this mean you're telling the whole Army about us?"

Winters widened his eyes. "Not a chance in hell. Not yet."

"So how are we supposed to be the best law enforcement around if nobody knows who we are?"

"Aw, come on, Major." Domino's smile disappeared. "This is a big deal. You gotta give us more free rein here."

"I don't have to give you shit. It's all right there in those packets." Winters pointed at the paperwork, which none of the pixies were remotely interested in reading. "Think of the next few weeks as a trial run. You go through your training, learn the ins and outs, get used to what's required of you, and don't screw anything up. Then, *maybe*, if your commanding officer feels he can trust you in the real world, you'll get to test it out."

"So it's like *Training Day*."

"What?"

Domino wiggled his eyebrows. "I *knew* it."

"It isn't the same as anything." Winters sat back in his chair and folded his arms. "And y'all won't be going through the same thing as all the other Army MPs either. All this is specific to the program *y'all* signed up for."

"Meaning?"

"Meaning you get a slightly new version. OIP MPs." The major frowned at the words, then tried to cover it.

Z snickered. "That's a mouthful, isn't it?"

Domino turned toward her and grinned again. "Oipcops."

"Hell, yes!"

"That's it, Major. You want something that just rolls off the tongue, it's oipcops. Go ahead."

"Y'all can call it whatever you want."

"Aw, come on." Z leaned forward and pointed at him. "Just give it a try."

"Oipcop," Domino prompted.

"You know you want to."

"No." Winters didn't look like he'd give in, but he did look like he was ready to get the hell out of there. "Whatever else y'all need to know before you get started is in those packets. I'd ask if you had any questions, but I honestly don't give a shit."

Domino stared at him. "Whoa."

The major stood, and Z slumped her chair. "Come on, Major. We should all be *excited* for our first official day on the job."

"On the oipjob," her cousin echoed.

"You're damn right. Trust me, I'm excited." Winters picked up his coffee, took another sip, and grimaced. "But if y'all have seriously burning questions, put 'em in writing."

The pixies snickered. "Burning, huh?"

"You know, I don't think paper is the best solution for that."

"Toilet paper, maybe, and that's a fifty-fifty chance."

Without stopping to engage in any of their ridiculous chatter, Winters headed for the door. When he opened it, Sergeant Packard was standing on the other side, fist raised in preparation to knock.

The young NCO staggered back, almost tripped over his feet, and struggled to keep his coffee from spilling.

"Where have *you* been?" Winters asked.

"Sorry, sir. I was looking for—"

"Thanks for the donuts, Sergeant!" Z shouted from the table.

"They were *so* good," Domino added. "Really helped with the whole hunger thing."

Packard looked like he was about to walk away, but his CO put him to work instead.

"Go find whoever's been assigned to set these yahoos up with their new assignment. Corporal Townsend can probably point you in the right direction."

"Yes, sir."

Winters didn't look at the pixies he'd just assigned. If he did, he didn't think he'd be able to walk away.

Better to put them in someone else's hands now. I got them through the first bit, and I'm not going to kill myself by sticking around for the rest of it.

As the major left him, Packard blinked at the three pixies.

Domino slapped his chest. "Check us out."

"We have *jobs*." Z barked a laugh. "Never thought *that* would happen."

"Oipcops, up top!" One by one, the pixies exchanged high-fives, ignoring Packard as they did.

When the sergeant remembered what he'd been ordered to do, he hurried away.

CHAPTER TWENTY-ONE

The pixies' first day on the job did not include any real training. Instead, another sergeant came to collect them from the room to get them settled into their new lives. He didn't give them his name, and he didn't say much as he guided the excitedly chattering recruits and their things into a van, then he climbed behind the wheel and drove them to their next destination.

The drive didn't offer any insight into what life at the base would be like for them. They passed concrete walls and buildings and electric fences and security towers. Occasionally, another vehicle passed them, but other than that, the place looked empty.

Z and her cousins couldn't resist asking every question that entered their minds.

"Hey, is that for keeping other people out or for keeping us in?"

"Is there a curfew?"

"Man, this place could really use some greenery. You like plants, Sergeant?"

"Where did you learn to drive?"

The sergeant stared ahead as if he couldn't hear a word even when Domino started making jokes about oipcops and reality TV and the pixies shrieked with laughter.

They pulled up in front of a low, square building standing separate from everything else. The van lurched to a stop, and the sergeant cut off the engine before opening the driver's side door and barking, "Get out."

"He *does* talk!" Domino held his hand out toward Echo. "Pay up."

Rolling her eyes, she reached into her pocket and pulled out what was left of her second donut.

By the time they'd left the van, their new guide was already on his way to the front door. There, he paused to wait for them, looking entirely too bored by his newest assignment. He also seemed unaffected by their large, glistening wings and the way sparks of silver, copper, or blue light burst from their fingertips.

He held up a single key before turning to unlock the door. Shoving it open, he stepped aside and gestured for them to enter.

"Oh, *wow*." Domino walked in first, taking in the whole thing with wide eyes. "Cool place you got here, Sergeant."

"I'm feeling a theme here," Z added. She followed him, Echo close on her heels. "You guys really need a new decorator."

The sergeant followed them in, then folded his arms. "Here's how this works. This place is yours."

"Ours?"

"You mean it?"

"Sergeant, that's an awfully big present."

"I'm not done." He'd either been briefed on how to handle them, or he didn't care about their antics, probably because his only job was to lead them here, and that was it. "That's your key. Don't lose it. You're on a highly secured area of the base. It's closed off from the rest of the base. For now. Until you hear otherwise, you don't get to step outside that gate."

"The super tall one with the signs that say, 'Caution, high voltage?'" Domino asked.

The sergeant blinked, then carried on. "This is where you sleep, shower, keep your shit, and turn in for the day. When you're not training or in your classes, I'd say it's better just to come home and stay out of everyone's way."

Z peered at the cramped kitchen and the chipped wooden cabinets lining the walls. "When's breakfast?"

"Whenever the hell you want, if you wake up early enough to eat before reporting for duty." The sergeant folded his arms and stared blandly across the barely furnished living room. "There's no mess hall 'cause you're not in Basic anymore. No access to the commissary on this part of the post either, so if you need something that's not here, write up a list and email it to Support."

"Who's that?" Domino asked.

"The contact info's all in that fun little packet you're holding. Shopping for requested items is only done once a week, so don't expect anything to get to you on demand. And these are *reasonable* requests only. Don't screw around with a bunch of bullshit nobody needs."

Only half-listening, the three pixies moved around the living room, taking in the bare walls and the old furniture and even older lamps lighting the corners.

Domino wrinkled his nose. "Can we redecorate?"

"I don't give a shit, but do it on your own time."

"How about painting the walls?"

"Ooh, is there central heating and air?"

"The place at least has hot water, right?"

"Do we have to pay for that? When do we even *get* paid?"

"Does this house come with an emergency button?"

"What happens if we run out of toilet paper in the middle of the night?"

"Ha, yeah." Domino choked on a laugh. "After all our *burning questions*."

The sergeant stood like a statue under the pixie's barrage of rhetorical questions. When they finally stopped and stared at him in expectation, he turned to leave. "Report to the yard outside the building tomorrow morning at oh-eight-hundred."

"Is that, like, a hard and fast rule with the whole timing thing?" Domino asked. "'Cause it might take a while to find the yard, Sergeant. I didn't see any grass outside."

The sergeant paused. "Little birdie told me you three get some extra-special punishment if you fuck this up, so I'd try not to fuck it up if I were you."

"A little birdie, huh?" Domino grinned and leaned toward the open door. "That's so cool. I didn't know humans could talk to birds too."

The sergeant rolled his eyes and opened the door.

"What's its name, Sergeant? Maybe I know this little bird."

The door shut behind him with a heavy click, and the pixies were left alone in their new home.

Domino blinked at the closed door. "Well, that was rude."

"Guys." Z spread her arms. "We have our own place."

"It smells funny," Echo murmured.

"I'm pretty sure everything in the Army smells funny." Domino skipped across the room and started going through the kitchen cabinets. "Whew. Especially over here."

Echo quirked her lips and scanned the living room. "Still no beds."

"We have the whole place to ourselves," Z replied, testing the couch cushions by thumping them with her fist. "And the whole rest of the day."

Domino looked up from beneath the kitchen counter he'd been investigating. "No place like home, right?"

"Right. So let's make this place home."

After decades of experience in packing up, moving at a moment's notice, finding a new place to lay their heads at night, and doing whatever they could to make said place feel like a home, Z and her cousins had become pros. For the rest of the day, their new "single-family home" was filled with a flurry of excitement, laughter, floating objects, magical light, and the kind of pixie-mischief activity that would have made even most other magicals run away to save their skin.

Their biggest hurdle, however, was finding there were other rooms in the squat little house and that three of them were intended to be individual bedrooms.

"Humans are *so* weird," Domino said, peering into one of the bedrooms. It was furnished only with a bed, nightstand, and small dresser. "How the hell do they expect us to sleep in separate rooms and get anything done while we're here?"

"I guess it's because that's what *they* do," Z suggested. "I don't know. Trying to keep up with why humans do anything makes my head hurt."

"Well, I'm not sleeping in a separate room."

Z fixed her cousin with a knowing smile and gestured toward the open bedroom door. "Nobody asked you to."

Before Domino could start in on the process of redecorating and rearranging, a loud bump came from the hallway on the other side of the house. He and Z hurried down the hall to see what was going on and found Echo emerging from the opposite hallway with the bed from the third bedroom raised in both hands above her head.

"Can't build good furniture for shit," she murmured before tossing the bed down into the empty center of the living room.

Domino pointed at his sister. "Good thing we have the skills to get it done."

"So let's get it done."

After that, their attention was focused on the house's living room and kitchen. Every other part of their new lodgings was ignored because they didn't have any use for it.

Blue, copper, and silver light streaked across the living room as Z and her cousins moved furniture to where they agreed it should go.

"No, no. A little to the right."

"Yeah, but then how are we supposed to get in?"

"Huh, then prop it up with one of those little tables."

"We need two."

"Where do you guys think is the best place to put the booby traps?" Echo called.

Z and Domino both turned to stare at her.

"Whoa. Where'd you get all those knives?"

Echo looked at the semi-sharp cutlery in her hands and shrugged. "The kitchen."

"Uh…" Z wrinkled her nose. "Maybe hold off on the booby traps for now, huh?"

"We're in a giant Army city surrounded by humans who don't want us here," Echo replied flatly, "And you don't think a little protection's gonna come in handy?"

"We have magic, E." Z pointed toward the kitchen. "That's gotta be enough for now. But how about this? If any of those humans from the rest of the giant Army city are stupid enough to try breaking in, *then* you can set up the booby traps."

The goth paused to consider the trade, then shrugged. "Fine. I guess."

The knives were systematically returned in a flash of silver streaks and pointy blade tips zipping across the living room to the kitchen drawers.

Z and Domino exchanged a quick, apprehensive look, then returned their attention to the biggest couch hanging below the ceiling in a shroud of deep-blue light.

"So." Domino cleared his throat. "A little more to the right?"

"Sure. Grab one of those nightstands."

Even with their scant breakfast of donuts, the pixies

were too focused on their work to think of anything else. They skipped lunch, determined to turn their concrete box into something they could call home.

Just after 6:00 p.m., they put the finishing touches on their new living arrangements and stood back to take it all in.

The entire living room had been repurposed into something that looked more like a fantasy playground for children than an actual home. All the bedroom furniture had been gathered there, and they'd had to get creative to place all three beds.

Echo's was off to one side, balanced precariously on a dresser. The other two beds were nestled along the far wall, with just enough space between them for a pixie to walk. Bookshelves balancing on small tables were stacked on either side of the beds, and the couch had been settled on top of those bookshelves to give the two beds a covered, cozy, play-fort kind of feel.

The kitchen table had been elevated halfway to the ceiling, and the legs propped up on stools and a side bench from the hallway. All the dresser drawers had been opened to provide extra balancing support, which also helped them double as easily accessible extra storage.

As the pixies gazed proudly at their handiwork, a few pieces of furniture groaned in protest at being used in a way for which they'd never been designed. With an enchantment and a lot of brainstorming, the whole conglomeration held with perfect integrity.

Domino sighed. "We're amazing."

"Not bad work, if I say so myself," Z added.

"Still smells," Echo murmured.

"Well, *you're* in a mood, aren't you?" Z scoffed and flicked her hand in the air. With a burst of deep-blue light, a flurry of hundreds of fuchsia flowers burst into existence just beneath the ceiling. They fluttered all around the living room, settling on awkward surfaces and toppling into the open drawers. They coated the old carpet covering the floor.

The slight stink had vanished, replaced by a light, pleasantly sweet fragrance.

"Happy now?"

Echo reached out to catch one of the last flowers, then shrugged. "Ecstatic."

"Great." Domino clapped his hands together. "Now we eat!"

"Did you find anything good in the kitchen?"

"Well, not *yet*."

Their kitchen had been stocked with nonperishable goods—dry noodles, canned vegetables, crackers sealed tight in tins, peanut butter, and an unmarked box filled with dozens of MREs.

When Domino found the ration packs, he let his imagination go to work. All the ingredients he felt were best for their first meal in their new home went into one giant pot on the stove, which he lit with magical fire instead of trying to figure out how to work the gas burners.

He served the resulting stew into bowls, and they took the reddish-brown slop into the living room. Picking a place around their crowded furniture setup, they gobbled down Domino's creation. Anyone else would have balked at shoveling down such a mishmash of food regardless of its calorie load.

Z and her cousins felt like royalty.

Looks like this is the end of us going hungry, Z mused, sipping the last of her meal straight from the bowl. *And it's happening in the Army. Who knew?*

With sated sighs all around, the pixies laid back to let their bulging stomachs settle. Domino whisked the dishes back to the kitchen sink with a flash of copper light, and the house fell into a full, content, and motionless silence.

After a few moments of quiet contemplation—or simple digestion without any thought involved—Z found herself thinking about their new job.

"Anybody else wonder why Dr. Goldbloom said we should be MPs?"

Domino looked at her from where he was sprawled on his bed. "Oipcops?"

"Yeah."

He tapped his lips and gazed at the ceiling. "I mean, if *I* were the doc, I'd say it has to do with our dedication to order, tidiness, and discipline."

A silent pause followed that before all three pixies burst out laughing.

"I hope I get to hit people," Echo murmured, punching a fist into her opposite palm. "I hope we go to arrest somebody, and they run, and then I get to pound them into the sidewalk."

Z raised her eyebrows and blinked at her cousin. "So again, why would the doc recommend we go into military policing?"

The goth shrugged. "Maybe she just saw our capacity for compassion and assumed it would be put to better use by challenging us to follow rules and punish rulebreakers while also having big hearts about it."

Z and Domino exchanged a confused look.

"Yeah. That's exactly what people think when they see you, Echo."

"Or maybe she just closed her eyes and pointed at a list of jobs." Echo shrugged. "Who cares?"

"Just curious. That's all." Overcome by a massive yawn, Z leaned sideways and dropped off the edge of the couch on which she'd been sitting. Fluttering her wings, she floated gently under the couch to settle sleepily onto her mattress. "Not like I'm a huge fan of turning in early or anything, but I'm beat."

"Gotta rest up for our first big day on the oipjob." Domino snickered. "That's totally catching on."

"I can't wait to throw somebody behind bars," Echo murmured sleepily. Two seconds later, she was out cold and snoring like a train.

Z lay on her back in her new bed and stared up at the underside of the couch. *If nothing else, Dr. Goldbloom thinks we're capable of taking this seriously. Now that we finally have a job, that's exactly what we're gonna do.*

CHAPTER TWENTY-TWO

It had been a long time since Z had dreamed, but tonight, she did, and when she did dream, it was the same thing.

She was back in her childhood home on Oriceran, in the large, healthy, purple-barked tree where the entire family of Thornbrooks had lived for generations. The place was brilliantly lit with tiny balls of enchanted light dangling under lush red leaves and bobbing in and out of doorways carved lovingly into the wood.

There was music. Dancing. Laughter.

The pixies didn't have a care in the world.

Until a stranger decided he cared too much about certain magicals' happiness on the plane and about what he could take from them after that happiness was gone.

Z relived everything in her dream. The music morphed into screams and shouts to get those too young or old to fight to safety. The healthy glow of enchanted pixie lights gave way to the terrifying roil of the wizard's green flames and the searing heat that came with them.

The Thornbrook pixies who were strong enough to

stand against the stranger put up a hell of a fight. It was as clear in her dream now as it had been that day over two hundred years ago.

Battle cries filled the air. Streaks of colored light darted back and forth. That dark, deep laughter as the wizard and his lackeys enjoyed the sight of the family scrambling to protect what it cherished.

"That's it. Fly away, little bugs. One way or another, I'll get what I came for."

Z's aunts had tried to pull her and her cousins to safety, but the rage boiling inside Z had overpowered her ability to think. Fueled by rage and refusing to sit back while others fought *for* her, she'd darted from the safety of the tree and into the battle.

She'd been old enough to stand with the rest of her family but still too young to understand what the consequences were going to be.

Standing beside the best pixie warriors her family had to offer, Z had redoubled her efforts to drive off the dark wizard and his two goons. It was the first time she'd truly let the full power of her magic go because, until then, she hadn't wanted anything as badly as she'd wanted to protect her family. Attack magic came so much more easily when she let the rage take over, and she'd truly thought she was doing the right thing.

But the rage and the fear of losing everything she loved had unlocked something else that night, something nobody had known or could have anticipated.

It was something that brought the battle for their beloved tree to a swift and disastrous end.

Z dreamed the whole thing in perfect detail as if she were reliving it second by second in real time.

The cool night air rushed across her skin as she darted from the tree and the lines of pixies defending their home. Her family shouting for her to come back. That it was too much for her to handle on her own. The flare of her magic building inside her in a way that made her feel like she could do anything in the world—and that no one could stop her.

She dreamed about the surprise in the dark wizard's eyes when her next attack did the exact opposite of what she'd meant it to do.

Somehow, her determination to drive off the attackers had opened up a new power. Her streak of dark-blue magic was meant to stick the dark wizard like the end of a sword, but when he recovered from a staggering blow, every bit of his magic had flared up with renewed force.

Stronger. Darker. Deadlier.

The green flames around him had roared to three times their previous height. The wizard's goons summoned spells with a flick of their hands that would have required much more effort to conjure.

Whatever power Z Thornbrook had held to protect her family, the simple act of having left the tree to charge the dark wizard had turned that power against her. She'd made him stronger, amplified the dark energy running through him, and realized what was happening much too late.

She dreamed of the blaze of churning green fire as the wizard sent one final, destructive attack at the Thornbrook tree.

There was fire everywhere. Screams. Smoke. Flickering

pixie lights that never quite made it beyond the confines of the blazing tree before they were snuffed out altogether.

The wizard's dark, bitter laughter could be heard through it all.

"What a fun surprise, little bug. Thank you for making this so easy."

Horrified, Z had sped back to the tree. She'd called for her parents, for her aunts and uncles, for her cousins and the elders and children barely fifty years old.

But she'd been far too late.

The only voices who responded to hers belonged to Domino and Echo. Z had found them huddled in one of the round pixie-sized gazebos carved into the higher branches.

She dreamed about pulling each of them by the hand as the smoke and green fire overwhelmed everything else—just before the dying tree splintered and fell and took the entire Thornbrook clan with it.

All but Z, Domino, and Echo.

The last.

Because of her.

"No!" Her scream tore Z out of her dream and pulled her back to the waking world. She sat bolt-upright, her chest heaving.

"Whoa, whoa. Take it easy."

That was Domino, but she couldn't find him because she was too busy ducking a blue-glowing plate whizzing toward her face. "What—"

"We're here, Z," Echo called as she flittered between a line of cutlery forming a swirling vortex in the center of the room.

"Just a dream," Domino added and managed to set a hand on her shoulder. "That's it."

Just a dream. Z swallowed thickly, then the reality of what was happening around her finally settled in. *No it's not. It was real...*

She stacked one piece of reality on top of another until she remembered who and where she was and what she'd done. Then the deep sadness settled in. With that sadness came the release of her magic on whatever was around her at the time.

Z drew her knees up to her chest and buried her face in them.

All the objects caught up in her dream-state freakout stopped in mid-air. The blue light surrounding them disappeared, and everything crashed to the ground.

Echo took that opportunity to dart toward her, stopping short just in front of her. She forced Z's head up off her knees, took her face in both hands, and held Z's gaze. "We're right here."

"Nothing's broken," Domino added as he assessed the state of the living room. "Nobody hurt."

That's not true. I hurt everyone.

Z sniffled, realized her cheeks were wet with tears, and pulled out of Echo's grasp so she could wipe them off. "Sorry."

"Nah, don't worry about it." Domino clapped a hand on her shoulder and gave her a reassuring little shake. "We know the drill."

"It's been a long time since the last one," Echo added with concern. "You okay?"

"Yeah," Z murmured. "I am now. Damnit, I thought that last one was, you know... The last one."

"Guess they come and go just like everything else." Domino fixed her with a crooked smile. "At least it happened *after* we moved into our house, right? I mean, if Sergeant Packard had seen this back in the mountain, he'd have melted into a puddle. No more Sergeant Packard."

They shared a weak laugh, and Z sighed. "That would've been a *little* worth it. Maybe."

"Wanna go blow something up?"

Z and Domino looked at Echo, neither surprised nor amused.

The goth shrugged and sat back on her heels at the edge of her cousin's bed. "The super fun sergeant who dropped us off here said we couldn't go past the electric fence. But he didn't say anything about not doing things *inside* the fence. They've gotta have some kind of armory here, right? So we fly in, grab something big, and go blow it up."

"Um..." Z tilted her head. "Why?"

"Always makes *me* feel better."

"Ha. Thanks but no thanks, Echo."

"Yeah." Domino kicked a foot against his sister's knee. "It's the thought that counts."

The pixies' multi-purpose living room went silent. Z wiped a final tear off her cheek and sniffed. "What time is it, anyway?"

Domino peered past the kitchen counter at the digital clock above the stove. "Six thirty-seven."

"Sorry."

"Hey, I was already waking up. Didn't expect to see a magical tornado, but that's all part of the fun." When the others didn't reply, Domino headed for the kitchen, avoiding the mess on the floor. "Who's hungry? I'll make breakfast."

"Nothing like stuffing your face with human food to get rid of a bad-dream hangover," Echo added, sliding off Z's bed next and heading to her side of the room.

"Sounds good, Dom." Z sat a little longer, wrapped in a tangle of sheets.

I wish I could forget about the whole thing as easily as they can. But even my cousins don't know what happened that night.

Taking a deep breath, she collected herself from the nightmare's aftermath and slid out of bed to get ready for the day. "Oh, Dom?"

"Yeah?" Cabinets banged in the kitchen.

"Leave out the canned sardines this time, huh? Tasted good last night, but we should probably try to make a good first impression on the oipjob."

"So, that means *no* sardines?" Domino paused, considering the implications of showing up for their first day with his breath stinking of fish. "You know what? I'll leave 'em off yours. Echo?"

His sister rummaged through her dresser to pull out yet another all-black uniform. "I like sardines."

"Got it. We're gonna *rock* this first day. Just you wait."

CHAPTER TWENTY-THREE

The simple act of getting ready for the day made it easier for Z to let go of the nightmare's lingering shadow.

Her cousins had always helped with that, too, mostly because they knew what was happening without having to sit down and hash it out again. Domino and Echo were a part of the nightmare because they'd been a part of that terrible day on Oriceran, the day Z had sworn to both of them that she would always keep them safe.

It was also the day they'd set out on their own, looking for a way to pass the gates from one planet to another and never look back.

For the most part, Z didn't but it was hard to do when the past reared its ugly head in her sleep.

It was also hard because she'd never told her cousins what she'd learned that night—that her magic hadn't fought against the dark wizard but had *magnified* it instead.

They don't need to know that part. They don't need to know our whole family's gone because I couldn't get a handle on my stupid feelings. We're together. We're on Earth. That's all that matters.

Not talking about it had served to protect them and their identities for the last two hundred years since she knew the wizard would stop at nothing to get his hands on her, just like he'd stopped at nothing to get his hands on the enchanted seeds the Thornbrooks were known for crafting and cultivating within their family tree.

She was sure he'd taken all those seeds when he'd destroyed her home, and part of keeping her cousins safe was making sure no one ever found out exactly who they were and where they came from.

News traveled fast in magical circles, even between planets.

Guess we made a pretty good call in the end. No dark wizard's gonna come looking for a superpowered pixie in the US Army, that's for damn sure.

With that thought, Z tugged on her uniform, laced up her boots, and ate the nameless mixture Domino had whipped up for breakfast. Her bowl was *sans* sardines, as requested.

"Huh. Tastes kinda like mashed potatoes."

"With jelly," Echo added.

Domino shoveled the rest of his food into his mouth and shrugged. "Yeah, I know it's missing something. I wanted to add oatmeal, but that's apparently not something the humans here think we'd eat. I guess I'll start a grocery list. With oatmeal."

His sister pointed at him and nodded curtly. "And ghost peppers."

"Ooh. And spinach dip." With a flick of his hand,

Domino pulled a pen and a pad of paper from one of the kitchen drawers. Both items zoomed across the room in a blaze of copper light until he snatched them from the air and started writing.

After that, a magical cleanup and dishwashing got the pixies' kitchen clean and sparkling. Then it was time to set out for their new lives as magical military police.

Domino strode to the front door, whistling a happy little tune.

Echo frowned after him. "I thought dwarves were supposed to do that?"

"Well, I feel good, and I'm off to work."

"It's, 'Off to work I go,'" Z corrected.

He pointed at her and grinned. "Exactly. Let's do it."

Z shot a quick glance at the single house key resting on the half-wall just inside the front door. Instead of grabbing it, she sent crackling blue light around the doorframe for a quick and easy security spell and called it good.

It wasn't a booby trap, but if anybody tried to mess with *this* home, Z and her cousins would know who'd done it and how to handle it.

For the next twenty minutes, the three pixies walked aimlessly over the concrete surrounding their little house, thoroughly confused as to how to carry out their first order of the day.

"I don't get it." Domino stopped in the middle of the road that wasn't quite a real road and spread his arms. "He said to report out in the yard."

"Well, a yard didn't just spring up out of the ground overnight," Z muttered. "Obviously."

"Did he want us to *make* it?" Echo wrinkled her nose. "I'm not doing hard labor."

"Maybe it's not *right* outside the house." Z turned in a slow circle, but as far as she could see, there was nothing but cement, darker cement, and a patch of asphalt a quarter of a mile out. "Guess we're hunting for a yard, then."

"I hope there's trees," Domino mused.

Under the cool, brisk morning air, the three pixies headed through the concrete jungle that was their newly assigned post. They didn't pass a single human, didn't hear a single vehicle engine humming in the distance, and only looked up at a loud jet streaking across the sky, a white stream trailing behind it.

When they got close to the patch of asphalt, Z pointed straight ahead. "There's another building. Don't see any green, though."

"Wait, is *that* a tree?" Domino leaned forward, squinted, then widened his eyes. "Nope. Can't tell."

"Well, it's the only thing out here, so let's check it out."

Domino hummed an aimless tune instead of whistling as they closed on the patch of asphalt. The lone figure in the distance turned out to be their commanding officer standing on this particular version of "the yard," waiting for his new recruits to show up.

"Z." Domino elbowed her in the side and lowered his voice. "That's a human."

"Yep."

"And I thought it was a tree."

"Maybe *the yard* is where they bury the bodies," Echo mused. "And grow new humans."

Z wrinkled her nose. "Are you sure that's how that works?"

The goth clammed up as soon as they were within hearing range of the human. He was tall and lanky with a shock of bright-red hair, and he stood alone in front of the single nearby building.

When he caught sight of the soldiers heading toward him—one wearing all-black against regulations and all three with their wings trailing behind them—he faced them and kept waiting. Only once did he pull his dark sunglasses down the bridge of his nose to make sure the new soldiers *did* have wings, and those were the source of the glinting reflection that had caught his attention.

Then he slid his sunglasses back up his nose, glanced at his watch, and squared his feet to clasp his hands behind his back. "You're late."

"Couldn't find the yard, sir," Z replied. "The name's misleading."

Domino leaned toward the man in uniform and whispered, "We thought you were a *tree*."

It looked like their CO was going to turn and leave. Instead, he nodded and looked the pixies over.

"Welcome to your MP training, Privates. I'm Captain Ordsen, your officer in the Military Police Corps, your instructor for the next few weeks, and your new boss."

"*Officer.*" Z and Domino exchanged wide-eyed glances to show how impressed they were, then Domino asked, "So, what do we call you?"

"Captain."

"Oh. Yeah, that works."

Ordsen scanned the expanse of concrete around them. "Any idea where Major Winters is?"

Domino barked a laugh. "You mean he's lost *again?*"

Z elbowed her cousin in the side and added, "No idea, Captain. He's just a real busy guy, you know?"

"Uh-huh." Ordsen sighed. "I guess we'll get started on our own, then. Let's go."

He turned to head toward the small building, obviously expecting his new trainees to come hurrying after him.

He'd never experienced "pixie time," which meant he got to the door only to watch the pixies exploring "the yard," searching every inch of concrete and asphalt with enthusiastic curiosity.

"We're ready to rock, Captain."

"Training starts now, and we're on it."

"Where's the playground, though?"

Ordsen raised his eyebrows. "What?"

"You know, the obstacle course. Ropes. Running. The wobbly bridge."

"Ooh." Z pointed at Domino and nodded. "I like that one."

"Right? Hey, we can climb a rope too if you want."

Fortunately for Captain Ordsen, his meeting with Major Winters had included a detailed warning of how obnoxious the Privates Thornbrook could be, so he wasn't taken as off guard by their questions as he might have been.

Still doesn't mean I'm grateful to Winters for shoving them on me. What the hell are we supposed to do with those wings?

He thrust open the door and gestured for them to go

inside. "This isn't Basic, Privates. No playground. I've got something even better."

As he'd expected, that got their attention. The pixies hurried into the small building set exclusively in the area sectioned off for the sole purpose of training, integrating, and overseeing new magical soldiers entered into the OIP.

In Army terms, that meant that Major Winters and Commandant Ordsen had been given bottom-of-the-barrel facilities.

When the captain closed the door behind him, the inside of the building was plunged into darkness. The sudden change in light made everyone blink and look around.

Removing his sunglasses, Ordsen crossed the small main room, flipped on the overhead lights, then went to the back, where a large whiteboard hung on the wall.

He gestured toward the three chairs and small tables in the center of the room. "Take a seat."

Z snickered. "For what?"

"Training starts now, Privates."

"Wait, I thought this was our *job*," Domino piped up. "You know, policing. Militarily."

Ordsen dipped his head in acknowledgment and jerked the cap off the first whiteboard marker. "It will be, once you complete your required class hours for each of the courses all new 31Es have to complete, and after you spend some time on base with the Police Department and the 31Bs tasked with enforcing military laws and regulations."

"Bs?" Z shot the captain a dubious frown. "You just said Es."

"Aw, did you get all your letters mixed up, Captain?"

"No. But thanks for your concern. You'll start off with the police department, and that's all you need to know. For now, it's classes and a fast track through whatever constitutes AITs for you three. You can't police if you don't know the rules or how to operate within them."

Ordsen snorted and graced the pixies with a ghost of a smile.

"Even militarily."

"You're kidding." Z folded her arms and glared. "You want *us* to do school?"

"*Doing school* is the only way you're getting out of this room, Private."

"And when do we get to, like, patrol the rest of the base and look for lawbreakers?" Domino asked.

Ordsen seemed surprised by that question, but he managed to take the whole thing in stride. "After school. Listen, I'm not a teacher by trade, so this is just as fun for me as it is for you. We're all here because we're all following orders."

Z sighed and took the lead in shuffling morosely to a desk. "Then I guess we have no choice."

"Correct. Any other reason to waste all our time, or are we ready to go?"

Domino groaned and pulled out the center chair so he could drop noisily into it.

Echo shrank, darted to the last open chair and table, and returned to human size on the chair with her arms folded.

"Great." Captain Ordsen looked them over, waiting for something to go wrong. All three looked unamused by their current situation, but that was the worst of it.

Well, I have no idea why Major Winters has such a problem with these guys. It's like sitting down with three teenagers who don't wanna do their homework.

Satisfied things hadn't started off on a much worse note, the commandant turned to the whiteboard and started their first lesson. "31E. Internment and Resettlement Specialist under the Military Police Corps. This is you in the foreseeable future *if* you're able to get through all your training without making me kick you out. Got it?"

"Internment Specialist." A smile spread across Domino's lips. "You mean like throwing people in jail?"

Ordsen turned to stare at the copper pixie, then blinked. "Let's just…start with the basics."

CHAPTER TWENTY-FOUR

Basics covered how to become Army MPs. Z and her cousins didn't pay particular attention to anything that didn't immediately grab their interest—like the types of privileges they would have as magical MPs and the excitement of apprehending and detaining *whoever they wanted* if there was any suspicion of misconduct, a threat to others, or the breaking of military law.

If they'd been graded on their ability to accurately move through the little question-and-answer sessions Captain Ordsen had prepared for them at the end of his two daily lectures, they'd have failed. Fortunately, the commandant's main goal was to build a rapport with his trainees until they reached the point where he felt comfortable enough to ask them a different type of question.

"Little bit of a change of subject," he started, then cleared his throat. "What can you do with those wings?"

"With these... Huh?" Domino scrunched his nose.

"Those shimmering things coming out of your back." Ordsen pointed at the appendages in question without missing a beat. "Don't tell me you had no idea they were there."

"Well, yeah, but no one's ever asked us what we can *do* with them."

"Now I'm asking."

"I mean, we can *fly*."

"Not sure they're good for much else, Commandant," Z added.

"Can you make 'em go away?"

All three pixies looked appalled by the question.

"*This* again?"

"Yeah, what is it with the Army asking us to chop off our wings?"

"That's not what I meant." Running a hand through his bright-red hair, the captain sighed and drew on his seemingly endless reserves of patience. "I mean, can you make it *look* like they're gone? You know, blend in with your surroundings."

"You mean like camouflage?"

Ordsen shrugged. "With humans."

"*Oh.*" The pixies all laughed, then Z slapped a hand on her small table before wagging a finger at their captain. "You should've just started *there*, Captain. You're talking about making them invisible."

"Sure."

"Easy-peasy." Domino snapped his fingers, and his copper wings shimmered, then vanished. At least, that's what it looked like.

Ordsen's eyes widened, then he sat back in his chair with a contented smile. "Now the rest of you. Let's see it."

Z and Echo both cast quick illusions to hide their

wings, only doing so because they were more curious about what their commander was getting at than offended by the request.

He looked from one pixie to the next, his approval growing.

"This isn't a forever thing, Captain," Z muttered. "We can't just keep these things hidden all the time. Not if you want us to do our jobs."

"Yeah, seriously," Domino added. "It's like having the squirts while trying to pour hot water into a tiny teacup."

Everyone watched him with confusion and disgust, but the copper pixie, his wings invisible, folded his arms and shrugged. "I'm just saying."

"Not all the time," Ordsen replied as he stroked his chin. "But you're gonna have to work on managing your duties while keeping those wing things in check *some* of the time."

"Why?"

"Because no soldier or officer in their right mind is gonna follow the rules when they're coming from three strangers with fucking *wings*. We gotta ease into the transition. Make sure you three can do your jobs and do them well before we bring more magicals into the program."

Domino lifted his chin and grinned. "You mean we're going *incognitive*."

"Incognito," Z corrected.

"Yeah. That."

"Something like that, sure." Ordsen nodded, then took a deep breath to continue with his little spiel.

But the pixies' minds were racing with what he'd just told them, and they couldn't focus.

"Wait, so you're turning us into spies."

"Are *all* MPs spies?"

"There somebody on this base we need to investigate right now, Captain?"

"Domino's really great at changing his face," Z added. "Or mostly his clothes. But it makes him look like literally anyone he wants."

"Aw." Her cousin flashed her a beaming smile. "Thanks."

"You're not doing anything like that right now," Ordsen cut in, determined to cut the sidetrack as quickly as possible. "But today was your last day of classes. Congratulations."

Echo lifted a finger and twirled it.

The commander snorted, then continued. "Which means it's time to walk you through our systems. Computer access, personnel files, radio surveillance. Everything an MP on this base has to keep an eye on, day in and day out. Because while you're here, keeping the peace within the Army, those systems are pretty much your lifeline. That and your training, but we're working with a different baseline as far as that goes."

"You mean…" Domino's eyes widened. "You're just gonna open up access to every single piece of information about every single person in the Army and how to *spy* on them?"

"Again, that's an overgeneralization, but essentially, sure. I guess." Ordsen looked more uncomfortable when he caught onto what was going through the pixies' minds. "Once you prove to me that you can handle that kind of authorization. This isn't about free rein. You can't just do whatever you want whenever you want and expect there to be no consequences. We have laws and regulations too, and we follow them. This is the Army, not the Wild West."

Z pointed at him and winked. "But it *is* Colorado."

"I guess." Frowning, Ordsen shook his head and stood from his chair. "We're done with the classroom, Privates. There's a vehicle parked out in the yard. I want you on it in five minutes."

"For what, sir?"

"To take a ride." With a sigh, Ordsen walked toward the bathroom in the hall, even less sure than before about what he was getting himself—and the entire Military Police Corps—into.

"Wait a second, sir," Z called after him. "How long do we have to wait before we're, you know, *on* the job?"

"Not long. Trust me." Ordsen took another step but was stopped again by yet another question.

"So when do we start?"

"For the love of— Give me five minutes and meet me out in the yard!" After that, Ordsen practically ran to the bathroom and slammed the door behind him.

Left alone in their classroom, the pixies looked at each other with growing anticipation.

"He said today."

"Pixie spies."

"We get to arrest *humans*."

After a moment of tense silence, all three pixies shrank and zipped across the room. Trails of magical light twirled and zigzagged behind them, and the front door burst open with a bang. From the bathroom until he reached the yard, Captain Ordsen had to listen to their high-pitched cackling.

Get sneak peeks, exclusive giveaways, behind the scenes content, and more. PLUS you'll be notified of special **one day only fan pricing** on new releases.

Sign up today to get free stories.

Visit: https://marthacarr.com/read-free-stories/

AUTHOR NOTES - MARTHA CARR
FEBRUARY 28, 2023

I've started a project answering questions for my son about my life. I realized after last year's fifth round of cancer, and then chemo this time that he was expecting me to die sooner rather than later. It's been a lot for him to deal with and there isn't much I can do to make it better, except tell him stories that I can leave behind – eventually. Hopefully, a long time from now. I'm going to let you guys listen in as well.

My author notes for this year are going to be answers to questions and all of you can get to know me better, too. Maybe inspire, maybe give you a laugh along the way.

Today's question is: Did you work while you were in college?

I started working when I was fifteen years old and it just kept going from there. In the house I grew up in, if you wanted something - anything - you had to go earn it yourself. There were a lot of odd jobs over the years. Working in a Barnes & Noble, cleaning houses (I remember a neglected basement that can still give me a shudder at the memory), as a nanny one summer for a family fleeing Iran after the Shah was ousted, working in a clothing store at the mall, at the University library, in the offices of a coal mining company. You get the idea.

By the way, that kind of scattershot is what happens when we tell our kids to be anything but what they want in their hearts. Writing wasn't on the acceptable list so I was always trying to make something, anything else, fit. Oddly, all those experiences probably helped me when it comes to thinking up different characters or plots.

But during college, the main job I had was as a waitress in a diner called, The Village. It was down on Grace Street across from a triple X adult theater on a narrow, two-lane, one-way road and just down from a Pizza Inn. My college roommate, Amy worked at the Pizza Inn and her job was to make pizzas in the window. When it was slow she would eat the dough and watch who was coming and going from the theater.

The manager of the diner took a dislike to me from the moment he met me, and hired me anyway. My existence rubbed him the wrong way and he let me know every chance he got. It was a bad habit of mine in those days to stay where I wasn't wanted and just endure. It really took a while for me to learn, there are better options out there - go find them. I was already paying for college on my own and an apartment with a roommate in let's say, a questionable building. There weren't a lot of people I trusted to ask questions or confide in, in those days and I was doing my best to get somewhere else where things might be better.

Again, it was all a whir of confusion while I tried to be something that would get approval outwardly, instead of honoring myself. Boy, if I could go back and talk to that girl I would be her biggest cheerleader and tell her, head straight for what you want. You're gonna do it in the long run, anyway and with a baby and still on your own. Might as well break out now and just be yourself. Your tribe is out there. These people are a tiny segment of the world. Miniscule, microscopic. Head out into the world.

But, I didn't and I stayed at that restaurant to pay the bills. It's the only job I ever had nightmares about. I'd have just gotten every table kind of happy and then I'd realize there was a vast field of tables behind me that I didn't notice till just that second. Woof. It can still make me take a deep breath and let it out slowly. It's also why I tip generously. Imagine running on your feet, getting yelled at by kitchen staff (that's the norm in a diner) and then being at the mercy of the patron and how much they decide to pay you.

Once there was a large group of women with a lot of special requests who all took out their calculators at the end. God forbid someone pay a dime more than they owed. Their tip was so small that the manager that day (a kinder one than that other guy), suddenly took it off the table and ran after the women, saying, "Here, you must need this more than she does." I was so grateful and amused that he did that.

Mostly, the customers were wonderful and there were a lot of regulars. It was a little tough to see the guys who drank themselves to a barely conscious state, wander back in, in late morning to nurse a cup of coffee and then repeat the process. But they were also some of the nicest guys and tipped well.

If there's a lesson from my days working during college, it's in the rear view mirror. I can endure anything and get through it - but why live like that? Like I have a million years to waste before really living. Get on with things and head for what you really want to be doing and with the people or person or both that you want to be doing it with. You will never regret that decision and even on the bad days, you won't hate what you do. Love you. Love, Mom. More adventures to follow.

AUTHOR NOTES - MICHAEL ANDERLE

FEBRUARY 22, 2023

Thank you for not only reading this book but these author notes as well!

Have you ever wondered why werewolves have a better rep than pixies?

I was thinking about this sine I have written about vampires, werewolves, zombies, magic users, magic users in space, witches etc. etc. etc.

Now pixies. Personally, I am having a blast with the deadly, scary pixies in another of my series, but they are a tiny part of the story.

It got me thinking.

If I had to create ten reasons you would want pixies in your army, what could I come up with?

I'm glad you asked.

TenReasons You Might Want Pixies in Your Army.

1. **They're small but mighty.** Sure, werewolves might be big and strong (and hairy and smelly), but have you ever seen the kind of havoc a tiny faerie can wreak? They may be small, but they're not to be underestimated. You don't want a pixies sword up your ass as a practical joke.

2. **They can fly.** I mean, come on! This one's a no-brainer (which is good for me. I'm running on half a brain today). Pixies have wings, so they can take to the skies and rain chaos on the enemy. Good luck trying to do that with a werewolf.

3. **They're masters of illusion.** Need to distract the enemy while you make a tactical retreat? Pixies have you covered. With their ability to create illusions and glamours, they can create all sorts of confusion and chaos on the battlefield.

4. **They're fast.** Werewolves might be speedy, but pixies can move even faster. With their quick reflexes and lightning-fast movements, they can dodge enemy attacks and zip around the battlefield with ease. Need to tell Corporal Buttercup to get his ass out there and lead from the front? Pixies are your go-to harassment comm.

5. **They're sneaky.** Need to get behind enemy lines undetected? Pixies are experts at sneaking around and staying hidden. They can easily slip past guards and sneak into enemy territory without anyone even knowing they're there. Try that with a massive wolf with glowing eyes and a body odor that even those without a good sense of smell will notice.

6. **They're great at reconnaissance.** With their ability to fly and their small size, pixies are perfect for scouting enemy positions and reporting back. Plus, they can do it without being seen or heard. Note: I realize that they aren't that great at long distances. So, if you need something from hundreds of miles behind enemy lines? Yeah, I'd have to give it to the werewolves.

7. **They're skilled negotiators.** Sometimes the best way to win a battle is to avoid fighting. Pixies are known for their charm and charisma, so they might be able to talk their way out of a conflict before it starts.

8. **They can heal.** Werewolves might be tough, but they're not known for their healing abilities for OTHERS (They heal themselves just fine). Pixies, on the other hand, have magical powers that can heal wounds and injuries, making them valuable additions to any medical unit in the military.

9. **They're versatile.** Pixies can do it all, from fighting on the front lines to sneaking around behind enemy lines to gathering intel and negotiating with the enemy. They're like a one-stop shop for all your military needs. Yes, I realize I'm grabbing a new line that is nothing but an aggregation of earlier ideas, but I'm running out of steam.

10. **They're just cool.** Let's face it, werewolves are overdone. Everyone knows about them and their "I turn into a big scary wolf once a month" thing. Pixies, on the other hand, are mysterious and

magical and just plain cool. Plus, they have wings, and who doesn't love that?

That's it. That is the best I can do. For those who are Team Werewolf, feel free to drop me notes in the reviews and give me your top three reasons werewolves would be better in the armed forces!

;-)

Chat with you in the next book.

Ad Aeternitatem,

Michael Anderle

MORE STORIES with Michael newsletter HERE: https://michael.beehiiv.com/

GET SMOKED OR GO HOME

They say she's not good enough for the family business. Maybe it's because she was meant for something better.

Sometimes what looks like the worst day ever, is the beginning of our best adventure.

Idina takes that first step into a new life and gets the hell away from them to forge her own future.

But her calling is the one thing they are the most against. She joins the military just like Uncle Rick. The other family outcast.

A new Warrior is about to find out the true roots of the Moorfield name. Nothing will ever be the same.

AVAILABLE ON AMAZON AND KINDLE UNLIMITED!

BOOKS BY MARTHA CARR

THE LEIRA CHRONICLES
CASE FILES OF AN URBAN WITCH
THE EVERMORES CHRONICLES
CHRONICLES OF WINLAND UNDERWOOD
SOUL STONE MAGE
THE KACY CHRONICLES
MIDWEST MAGIC CHRONICLES
THE FAIRHAVEN CHRONICLES
DIARY OF A DARK MONSTER
I FEAR NO EVIL
THE DANIEL CODEX SERIES
SCHOOL OF NECESSARY MAGIC
SCHOOL OF NECESSARY MAGIC: RAINE CAMPBELL
ALISON BROWNSTONE
FEDERAL AGENTS OF MAGIC
SCIONS OF MAGIC
THE UNBELIEVABLE MR. BROWNSTONE
DWARF BOUNTY HUNTER
ACADEMY OF NECESSARY MAGIC
MAGIC CITY CHRONICLES
ROGUE AGENTS OF MAGIC
WITCH WARRIOR
THE AGENT OPERATIVE
BIG EASY BOUNTY HUNTER

OTHER BOOKS BY JUDITH BERENS

OTHER BOOKS BY MARTHA CARR

JOIN THE ORICERAN UNIVERSE FAN GROUP ON FACEBOOK!

BOOKS BY MICHAEL ANDERLE

Sign up for the LMBPN email list to be notified of new releases and special deals!

http://lmbpn.com/email/

For a complete list of books by Michael Anderle, please visit:

www.lmbpn.com/ma-books/

CONNECT WITH THE AUTHORS

Martha Carr Social
Website:
http://www.marthacarr.com
Facebook:
https://www.facebook.com/groups/MarthaCarrFans/

Michael Anderle

Website: http://lmbpn.com

Email List: https://michael.beehiiv.com/

https://www.facebook.com/LMBPNPublishing

https://twitter.com/MichaelAnderle

https://www.instagram.com/lmbpn_publishing/

https://www.bookbub.com/authors/michael-anderle

www.ingramcontent.com/pod-product-compliance
Lightning Source LLC
LaVergne TN
LVHW041755060526
838201LV00046B/1011